# THE PIRATE QUEEN
# DARK TIDES

## BOOK TWO

By
Candace Osmond

CANDACE OSMOND

Cover Work by Majeau Designs
Facebook.com/MajeauDesigns

# DEDICATION

For Corey, the king to my queen.

# ACKNOWLEDGMENTS

I'd like to thank Majeau Designs for another amazing work of art for this series, and for taking the time to create the custom chapter headings. I love them! I'd also like to thank my beta readers for helping me make this book what it is. And the biggest thank you goes to all the readers who devoured book one, and made it soar to the tops of the charts. Without you, there would be no book two.

# CHAPTER ONE

You get used to waking up to the rolling of the sea. It lulls you to sleep at night and softly coaxes you awake each morning. I used to hate it. But after a while, sleeping on land in a big, comfy bed, it's like being held in place by the world, unable to move. Everything's too still. The best is sleeping up on deck in the dead of Summer, blanketed by the heavy August humidity but cooled by the twilight chill that creeps in. Sleeping up there is the wise when you share a ship with twelve burly pirates.

A moan escaped my body as I rolled over, my hair tousling in the morning wind. But a sudden pain in my shoulder forced me to roll back. Did I fall asleep next to Finn? Did the giant Scotsman crush my shoulder in the dead of night? I attempted to turn over once more, but the pain was too much, I could barely move. But, something else was off. Everything felt... wrong. There was no gentle heaving of the ship. The wind didn't carry with it the misty drops of seawater. I felt anchored. Steady. The same as when I'm on land. Then I remembered, the visions rushing back to me like a movie stuck on fast forward.

"Henry!"

I bolted upright, panic and adrenaline suddenly alive in my veins, pushing the blood throughout my body with a hard rush. A quick look around told me that I was alone, but also dumped on the side of a lumpy hill. More memories flashed through my mind; the Celtic witch chanting, the glowing bottle, a raging fire, then Henry's desperate face as I...

I craned my neck to search again, trying to find some resemblance of my where I was... or *when* I was. My eyes collected the information as if it were picking crumbs off the floor; rocky hillside, the ocean in the distance, the strange metallic smell in the air. More images flashed across my vision; Maria's sword, the snow globe. My head shot upwards and I found the looming stone structure far above me.

Signal Hill.

I was nestled on a nook in the side of the steep cliff that descended from Signal Hill, at least fifty feet from the road above. I had to get up there but, as I lifted the flap of my red pirate's coat, I discovered that the whole left side of my torso was soaked in blood and my arm hung from it like a sack of meat and bones I'd slung over my shoulder. But I had to get off the hill. I had to find help and get back to Henry.

If he was still alive.

No. I shook those thoughts from my brain. He was still alive, he had to be. I had to believe that, hold on to it with certainty. I forced my body to move. My good arm grabbed a rock nestled in the hillside above my head and hauled myself up. My limbs shook as I held my grip and straightened my legs, every ounce of my energy coming to the surface and burning up faster than I could summon it. Finally, in an upright position, my body relaxed against the grassy hillside, completely spent from the couple of feet I'd moved. My eyes slowly scanned upward until they reached the top where I could vaguely see the stone railing that lined the road to the Signal Hill tower. It felt like light years away.

"Help!" I screamed. "Anyone!" But my attempts were futile. The landmark had been cleared of sightseers. I wanted to cry but it would have been a waste of what little energy I had. No one was going to help, I had to get off the hill myself.

"Come on, brain," I told myself, "work." I couldn't pull myself up the hill, that was made pretty clear after my weak attempt. Then, I noticed the evidence of wear marks in the grass in the short distance. My eyes followed the overgrown footpath as it made its way along the side of the hill and, eventually, led to the road above. Relief flooded my body. I could slowly follow the trail, step by step, without having to expel what little energy I possessed. It would take longer, but at least I could be certain I'd reach the top.

Bit by bit, I pushed my feet along the wear line in the grass, slowly inclining as I went. My weak and damaged body demanded to stop and take breaks every few feet, which I gladly obliged, knowing I was making progress. Eventually, as the sun entered a high point in the mid-morning sky, I reached the rocky road that led the way to the tower and grabbed hold of the stone railing, its rough surface scrapped the palm of my hand as my defeated body pushed its weight down. I was fainting, collapsing from the use of energy I didn't have. But a voice rang out from nearby and I craned my neck to see a man running toward me, assuring that I'd be okay, and allowing me to let go. The last thing I remembered was my heavy body hitting the hard ground below me, but it was okay. I'd made it.

\*\*\*

You always see those scenes in movies or on TV when someone is experiencing a traumatic event and they're being rushed to the hospital. Everything happens in short, vivid clips of faces, flashes of light, and voices telling them they're going to be okay. But you never stop to think that it's like that in real life.

It is. But worse.

My mind sank under the surface of my consciousness, only coming up for air now and then. It was a way to deal with pain. The excruciating pain that came with the vivid clips of faces, flashes of light, and everyone telling me it's going to be okay. I remembered the ambulance arriving at Signal Hill and hands, so many hands, coming from every which way, grabbing and pawing at my body to remove my blood-caked clothing. Every movement, every tug and pinch sent volts of pain and forced agonized moans from my body, but it all stemmed from my shoulder. I screamed at some poor paramedic as she accidentally ripped my jacket further and grabbed her by the throat. They restrained me after that.

The drive to the hospital was an endless pattern of questions followed by poking and prodding. I felt a hand grasp my face as its fingers lifted my eyelids and shone a light inside. "Miss, do you know your name?"

"C-Cobham," I squeaked out, "Dianna Cob—ow!" I'd thought for a moment that they caught fire to my shoulder wound and I realized that the other paramedic had just begun cleaning it.

"Dianna," the other woman spoke, "I need to know what happened. How did you get this wound?" she asked. More poking and prodding.

"Where did you come from? How did you get to Signal Hill? Who did this to you?" The questions never ended, and my head spun with all the answers I couldn't speak in this reality. They'd think I was insane, and the last thing I needed was to end up at the Waterford.

"Could an animal have done this?" the male paramedic asked her.

She leaned over my body and examined the gash across my shoulder. "No, I mean, maybe?" she replied, "But what kind of animal? Nothing like that around here."

She wasn't wrong. Maria Cobham was an animal from another time.

Before we reached the hospital, I fell unconscious, whether from the pain or exhaustion or meds they'd given me, I had no idea. But my mind fluttered awake in short spurts. Being moved to a stretcher. Blackness. Doctors rushing me down a hallway as the blinding lights passed overhead in a nauseating pattern. Blackness. Being moved to a flatbed and more questions I could never answer. Blackness.

When I finally awoke again, it felt like it had been unusually long since I'd last been alert and my brain lagged with a strange fogginess. Pain meds. I vaguely recalled the similar feeling when I'd had my appendix removed a few years ago. The annoying beeping sound nearby throbbed in my brain and the sunlight filling the room hurt my eyes.

"H-hello?" I choked out. Like a drunk person, I tried to move and shifted enough to find a call button next to my bed and rang for a nurse. It only took a few seconds for someone to show up.

"Well, good morning," the woman greeted as she went straight to the machines and IV bags stationed next to me, checking them over and glancing down at the chart in her hands. "You're the talk of the town, Miss Cobham."

An agonized moan crept out of my throat. "What? Why? Where am I?"

"You're in St. Clare's Mercy in St. John's, girl," she told me and began checking my shoulder dressing. "You were found near Signal Hill, collapsed on the ground and covered in blood. You've got the strangest wounds. Do you remember what happened?"

I tore my gaze away from her and stared out the window, blinding sunlight be damned. "Someone attacked me with a knife," I told her, hoping it would be enough to satisfy the police.

"Jesus. Must have been some knife. You're lucky they found you when they did. You lost a lot of blood," she informed me. "I'll go grab the doctor now and you can chat with him."

"No, I'm fine, really, just tell me where my things are, and I'll get out of here," I pleaded.

I could see the pity she felt as she cocked her head to one side and pursed her lips. "Oh, honey, you won't be getting out of here anytime soon. You just had major surgery to fix that shoulder of yours." She let the words settle on my ears. "You'll be here for a few days for observation. Is there anyone I can call for you?"

Yes, but he lives three-hundred-years in the past. "No, thanks," I told her but then remembered. "Wait, yes. My aunt. She lives in Rocky Harbour. Mary Sheppard. I... I don't know her number off-hand and I don't have my cell phone."

The nurse patted my hand and smiled. "No worries, Dianna. I'm sure it won't be hard to find her number. Rocky Harbour ain't that big."

"Thanks."

"I'll go grab the doctor for you now, and I'm sure the police will be in to visit you and get your statement."

She left me, and the silence of the room magnified against the annoying beeps of machines that surrounded me. A quick assessment told me that my one arm was useless. The surgery left it numb and they'd wrapped it heavily before setting it up in a high-tech sling of some sort. IV needles tugged at the insertion points in both my arms, a gross and uncomfortable sensation.

I tried to relax as I turned my gaze to the big, bright window next to me, letting the sunlight burn my eyes and numb my brain. Being here, in this... time, it didn't feel real. More like a super vivid and painful dream. I wanted nothing more than to wake up and find Henry in bed next to me. My gorgeous, rugged, sweet pirate king. I felt a tear escape the corner of my eye as I thought of what may have gone down after I disappeared. Did they win? Did Eric and Maria kill the men I loved? My family?

"Good morning, Miss Cobham," a male voice spoke as it entered the room. I turned my head to find a doctor, a short and balding man with a wide smile. "It nice to see you awake and responsive."

"Yeah, I'm not sure I agree," I replied and winced when I tried to move my arm.

"Best not to move it for a few days, let the flesh heal before practicing any mobility," he told me and rested his bottom on the edge of my bed. He pulled out a chart and began to examine the papers. "So, the surgery went well. You should have a full recovery and most, if not all, use of your shoulder will return with lots of rest and self-care." He paused and searched my face for a reaction. I could barely muster up a half-smile. "Dianna, aside from your shoulder, you were badly injured, dirty, and very confused when they brought you in. Can you tell me what happened? Where you were?"

My mind raced as it scrambled for reasonable answers that would pass as sane. "I… I'd been out for a walk one evening and someone attacked me with a knife."

He nodded thoughtfully. "And why were you dressed in strange clothing?"

I shrugged and winced from the pain. "I have an obsession with old-world stuff?"

The doctor hummed and hawed at my weak answers. "We thought, perhaps, you'd been under the influence of narcotics, but the tests came back negative which was good, giving your condition."

"My condition?"

He grinned and flipped to a new page on the chart. "Yes, dear, it was almost too early to tell, but you're pregnant. Hardly two weeks."

Emotions boiled in my stomach and began to rise, forcing their way up to my throat where a silent cry escaped my lips. I could feel the blood pooling in my face as tears ran from my eyes. No, how could it be? Not only did I lose the love of my life, but I was stuck in a different time, far away from him, and pregnant with his child. A child I could never give answers to when they asked about Daddy. A child I would have to raise on my own. A child that Henry would never get the chance to see, or touch, or kiss.

The doctor ripped a few tissues from the small, yellow box on the side table and handed them to me. "I take it you weren't aware?" he said, and I just shook my head. "Well, Dianna, given your injuries and your new condition, I highly suggest you stay here for a few days for observation. But we've called your aunt and she'll be here tomorrow, so at least consider staying overnight?"

"Okay, yes, thank you," I sputtered out over tear-drenched lips.

"Excellent," he replied and gently pat my leg before standing. "The police are outside, they'd like to ask you a few questions about your attacker. Is that alright? Are you up to it?"

"Yes," I said, "Although, I don't have much else to say about it. I never, uh, seen the man's face or anything."

Lies. All lies. I'd never be able to tell the truth of the adventure I had or the tragic loss I just experienced. It's all a secret burden I'd have to carry with me for the rest of my life. My stomach clenched as I realized the painful untruths I would now have to live with every single day.

The police came in, two officers, a male and female, and they asked me a series of questions that I gave short, vague answers to. Why was I out so late by myself? Why was I wearing strange clothing? Could I describe my attacker's face? What did the weapon look like? I didn't give them much to go on, but enough to keep them looking long enough to call it a cold case and just file it away.

After they'd finally left, I laid my head back on the pillow and fell asleep while I waited for Aunt Mary's arrival. It was a dark, empty sleep. No dreams. It was the best I could hope for because I never wanted to face the reality of what my life was becoming.

# CHAPTER TWO

"Tell me who she is, Henry!" Maria screamed at me, her ragged breath spitting all over my bloodied face. It'd been a day now. A day in this Hell with the devil herself. A day with my limbs bound and my body beaten for answers I would never give.

A day without my Dianna.

She threw another blow to my face. God, that woman had the strength of an ape. My mouth filled with the warm taste of iron and I spat it in her face. "Go back to Hell."

Her expression twisted into a broken grin; half

enraged, half conniving. I always thought it was as if two beings resided within Maria; good and bad, sane and insane. The woman should be locked up and studied.

I watched as she turned a metal poker over in the fireplace, waiting for its tip to glow red. "Where did she come from, Henry?"

I remained silent.

"You protect her, yet she's gone," Maria continued, prying around the outside. In a moment of weakness, I let a pained expression flicker across my face. But she caught it. "She's gone, left you behind for me to gather up the pieces. No one can love you as I love you, Pet."

"You haven't the slightest idea of what love is," I muttered.

Her brows raised in surprise. "And you claim to?"

I refused to answer. It would only give her the tool she needed to dig deeper. If Maria knew that I loved Dianna, it would be the end. But, perhaps, that would be for the best. An end. *The* end. But part of me feared too greatly that she'd find a way to Dianna's future, to destroy the one thing I loved, and I couldn't bear the thought.

"I'll get it from you yet," she half-whispered as she backed away, a disturbing and thoughtful look on her face.

"Get what?" I screamed at her.

I still didn't quite understand what it was she was truly digging for. The woman insisted on knowing who Dianna was, for obvious reasons. We all watched as the air around my beloved came to life and dragged her through time. The memory of her reaching out to me, my hands straining to get to her, the cold void left behind in her absence... as if she were never really there to begin with... it all flashed through my mind. Sharp, painful memories. Everyone stood frozen in shock and disbelief, only I knew what had truly happened. But the disbelief still struck me, nonetheless. She was gone, right before my very eyes. Taken away from me. The fact that she was safe, my only comfort.

Maria left the room and shut the door behind her, leaving me in the dark once again. My left eye had swollen shut, rendering me partially blind, but what did it matter? If the beast didn't pry the information from me she sought... I'd be a dead man in a matter of days.

I could only hope.

# CHAPTER THREE

Dreams are a funny thing. They can be alive with color and gorgeous imagery or dark and empty, void of... anything at all. I think it depends on what you're going through in life, the actions, the emotions, it all carries through into your sleep. The loss of Henry was a pain that had been thrust upon me and weighed my body down like a concrete slab. I wanted to feel nothing, to push the pain away and let the force of the slab crush me alive.

The very thought of living a life of secrets and lies was unbearable. I'd lost very little when I first traveled back in time. Just a boring, blank page in my life's story. But back there, back with Henry and Finn and the crew… my story began to write itself and the pages were alive with vibrancy. Now, I had to rip those entries out and pretend they'd never happened, to fill in the blanks for everyone around me and live a lie. I had to raise a child who'd never know their father, or that they were conceived 300 years ago.

I laid on a cold floor, darkness all around me as the weight of the concrete slab slowly squeezed the life from my body. I wondered if that was how my mother felt all those years? To be stuck in the future, so far away from her home and life. Did she really love my father? Did she love me? I shook the impossibility from my brain. Of course, she loved me. I knew it like I knew blood flowed in my veins. But she'd spent the better part of my life searching for a way home. That house, my house, a museum of archived things; trinkets, books, scrolls, enchanted items… if there were a way back she would have surely found it, wouldn't she?

Suddenly, a bright yellow light sparked to life on the edge of my vision. I craned my neck to see it. As the light grew and spread, an image of a room appeared. My mother's office. The light filled the dark space of my empty dream and the concrete slab slowly melted away. I stood and walked toward the center of the glow and stepped into the room. Surrounded by boxes and chests, a realization dawned on me.

A way back.

If there were a way to get back to Henry, the answer would be there, amongst my mother's things. Maybe Mom just never got the chance to search through it all before she died. It's there, it has to be there. I felt a hand gently caress mine as it took my fingers and twisted them in theirs. I looked to find my mother, standing by my side.

*"You can find it, baby,"* her music-box voice told me. *"Find a way back."*

An odd sense of hope-filled my chest and the room became too bright for my eyes. My mother and everything around me imploded with the never-ending glow and I was dragged to the surface of reality. But I didn't mind, I carried with me the hope of getting back to everything, to my life.

Back to Henry.

*** 

I awoke with a strange burst of energy, my mission bright and clear in my mind. Get out, go back to Rocky Harbour, find a way home. I repeated that over and over all morning while the kind nurse helped me bathe and get dressed. Waiting for Aunt Mary to show up was killing me. There was nothing keeping me there, I had to go.

I sat upright in bed, freshly dressed and ready to go, my insides bouncing with excitement because I knew Mary would have completed the seven-hour drive any moment. It was sometime after lunch when I heard footsteps approaching outside my open door, the distinct sound of Mary's voice speaking to someone, and tore the blanket off my legs to hop out of bed. But my joy was crushed when I saw who she brought with her.

"John?" I squeaked, my blood running cold as I slowly slipped from the hospital bed.

He entered the room behind a guilty-looking Mary and lunged forward to embrace me. His big arms held me, and I was frozen, stunned, totally confused at what was happening.

"Jesus, Dianna, where have you been? We've been worried sick." Finally, he pulled away to look at my face and, I swear, seemed as if he were about to kiss me.

Dodging the gesture, I wiggled from his grip and stepped back. "What are you doing here?"

"He came with me," Mary spoke up. "After you went missing, I called John from your cell phone to see if you'd maybe skipped off back to Alberta or something. After a couple of days, when you never turned up, John flew down to help with the search."

I failed to hide the confusion and disgust on my face. "Search?"

Mary put a hand on my good shoulder. "Yes, dear. Dianna, you've been gone *nearly a month*, no trace of where. No note. Nothing. My God, where have you *been*?"

I backed away and shook my head. It was too much. "I-I don't—"

"Dianna has experienced some trauma," the doctor piped in. "Her memory of what happened could be foggy, at best. I'd advise you to take her home, let her rest, recover. She's been through a great deal, and she'll put all the pieces together on her own terms. In time."

I couldn't look any of them in the face. The doctor was right, I'd been through a lot. But I remembered it all, the memories as sharp as the blade that had cut through me.

After the doctor signed my release papers, the nurse gathered my things in a large plastic hospital bag and handed them to Mary. My aunt opened the bag and peered in, and I knew the sight of my dirty pirate's coat and old trinkets would arouse questions. She reached in and began to pull out a gold chain, the one that held a large ruby stone and I snatched the bag from her hands.

I hugged the plastic satchel tightly to my chest with my good arm, the salt of the sea and the stench of The Devil's Heart wafting up to my nose. The sensation brought tears to my eyes. All that remained of the life I left behind was held within it. John tried to be chivalrous and take the large, heavy bag for me, but I held on like a crazed junkie.

The whole way home was like that; John trying to be nice, doing things for me. Racing ahead to open doors, helping me into Mary's car, putting on my seatbelt. I refused to speak to him, the sting of our breakup never healed, I never got closure, and now he was picking at the scab I never realize had formed. I sat in the backseat, the precious bag still clutched tightly to my chest, while Mary drove with John in the passenger seat. They chit-chatted back and forth like old friends, and my mind fought to process the scene. It felt unnatural.

This was going to be a long seven hours back to Rocky Harbour.

***

I'd fallen asleep along the way, a fact for which I was grateful. I couldn't stand listening to John's voice and feeling the tension emanating from Mary. She was dying to bombard me with questions, that much I could tell. I'd have to think of something to tell her, eventually. Something to placate her, to stop the endless questions I knew awaited me.

I was jostled awake when the car began traveling down a bumpy road and I knew we were almost home. The sun had begun to set, and the outline of my house could be seen through the front windshield. My breath caught at the sight of it. Sheets of plywood covered the side facing the ocean, the side of the house that was destroyed during the tidal wave that stole me away.

"A few of your cousins got together and put up the plywood, but there's a lot of work to be done," Mary told me and caught my eye in the rear-view mirror, taunting me to give her answers. "What a strange thing, a massive wave like that only reaching as far as here. None of the neighbors even felt it."

The car came to a stop and John scrambled out to open my door. He offered his hand, but I ignored it and tried to hide the struggle of getting out of the back seat myself. "Yeah, it must have happened after I… left."

Mary stared at me from the other side of the car, her eyes barely clearing the top of it, but they bore into me, drilling for answers. "So, you weren't here when this happened? Where did you go when you *left*?" I could hear the disbelief in her tone.

"Maybe we should let her rest," John cut in, "Remember what the doc said."

Mary grumbled something under her breath and we entered the house. I expected a mess, but the sight of the main floor shook me. Once soaked items and boxes stacked off to the side, now dry and warped from the water that had found its way in. The musty scent of water damage hung heavy in the air. All the furniture had been pushed into the kitchen, leaving nowhere to sit downstairs. God, it felt like another lifetime since I'd been there.

"What's the state of mom's office?" I asked desperately. "Did anything get wrecked?"

"No, seems to be fine," Mary replied and handed me a new key. "Aside from a few boxes that got wet." She paused thoughtfully, chewing on her bottom lip. "But I 'magine you'll be going through most of it anyway, won't you?"

My eyes widened. There was an underlining tone

to her words as if she somehow knew my plans to find a way back. Her eyes searched deep into mine, looking for confirmation of what she thought she knew.

"I can help with that," John cheerfully offered.

I cringed. "What do you mean? Aren't you going back to Alberta?" I asked. "I'm here, you found me. Mission complete."

John was nothing if not determined in his ways. Always was. He continued to plaster on the big, friendly smile as he helped me out of the hospital-issued sweater. "Are you kidding? I'm not going anywhere. Not without you."

I opened my mouth to protest but Mary beat me to it. "Get some rest, first. Worry about putting the house back together later." She turned to leave but stopped at the door. "Oh, and your little cousin Samantha is reopening the bakery tomorrow if you want to venture over and talk to her. Now that you're home, I don't know what you want to do with it."

My brain flipped through memories of my distant family. "Samantha? The one who went to the same culinary school I did?"

"Yeah, she's a fancy pastry baker now," Mary confirmed and shot me a grin, "She could do wonderful things with that bakery, Dianna. Don't make her shut it down."

"I wouldn't—"

Mary waved her hand. "We'll talk tomorrow, get some rest." She shut the door behind her, leaving me alone with John who was waiting like a puppy in the kitchen.

I walked over to him, my beloved plastic bag still clutched to my chest. I was dying to scuttle off into a dark corner and go through its contents.

"John, seriously. What are you doing here? You're not my boyfriend."

"I know, I know," he admitted as a hand nervously rubbed the back of his neck. "But I was. I completely fucked this up. I can't believe what a jerk I'd been, not appreciating what I had, what *we* had." He stepped closer and tried to take my bag again, a kind gesture, I knew, but I still flinched and refused to let him have it. "Okay, I get it. You've been through hell and back. I can't even begin to understand what must have happened to you. But, please, let me be here. Let me help. I don't want anything from you."

My head shook, and tears welled in my eyes. It was all his fault. If he hadn't cheated on me, I wouldn't have stayed here. I wouldn't have drunk too much rum and went through my mother's things where I found the ship-in-a-bottle. But, then, how could I possibly hate him for sending me down a path that brought me to Henry?

"What can you possibly do, John? What about your job?"

"I haven't taken a vacation in four years," he told me. "They owe me this time off. I explained the situation, my boss understands." I watched as he began pulling the old leather sofa from its upturned position in the kitchen and dragged it into the living room with ease. "I'll sleep here."

I moaned and rolled my eyes before turning toward the stairs. "I'm going to bed."

"Fine," he cheerfully called out to me. "I'll be right here if you need me! I'm not going anywhere," and then added, after I failed to respond, "G'night!"

I hauled my legs up each stair, taking my sweet time for that was all my body allowed. My energy was spent, and my wounded shoulder began to throb as the recent dose of pain meds faded away. I entered my old room, boxes and junk still stacked everywhere, and cleared a spot on the bed where I let my body sink.

I rolled onto my back, my good arm still wrapped around the plastic bag, and stared at the ceiling. The glow-in-the-dark stars from my childhood still littered the stucco surface and I recalled the day Mom helped me put them up. She held me on her shoulders as I reached up and stuck each one in place. That night, she slept in my bed alongside me as we laid there and admired the faint neon glow that hung overhead.

I wiped a tear that escaped my eye and moaned as I sat up to reach for the pill bottle in my pocket. I popped some more pain meds and dumped the contents of the plastic bag out on the bed in front of me. The strong stench of seawater and my own sweat wafted up to my face and my heart tinged with pain. I smoothed the dirty, bloodstained jacket out and my fingertips ran over the fresh tear that ripped across the left shoulder. Images of my last moment with Henry flashed through my mind like a movie brought to life on a screen before me.

Poor Charlie, my sweet boy. The life draining from his body as Maria let it fall to the forest floor by her feet. The sick and twisted look on her face as I choked on a scream. The light of the fire catching her sword as it swung toward me. And then... Henry's face. The pain I witnessed sear across it as the threads of time claimed my body and dragged me away from him.

I cried then, finally. It all came out, crashing to the surface like a dam giving way to the years of pressure. I couldn't stop it if I wanted to. Ugly, heavy sobs erupted from my insides as I continued to pick through the items on the bed. Trembling fingers brushed against the brown, blood-covered leather boots.

And then the clothing that Nathaniel had given me at The Thirsty Trout, where Henry and I first made love. I carefully smoothed them out and laid the garments over the jacket, only to find my necklace buried underneath. Smiling, I grabbed the gold chain, pulling it toward me, and held the large ruby tight to my chest. Henry's raspy voice rang clear in my ears.

*I love you, Dianna*, he'd told me down in that cave, the very first time he'd professed it.

I looped the necklace around my head, letting it fall and rest on my chest as I leaned over and snuggled up to the pile of clothing next to me. My hand gently rubbed my stomach, the sudden recollection that a little person was growing inside. Henry's little person. I wanted to cry again but couldn't find the strength to do it. The effects of the pain meds were kicking in and my eyes threatened to close, so I wrapped my fingers around the pendant and gave in to the heaviness of a deep sleep that washed down over me.

\*\*\*

For the first time in forever, I'd dreamed of nothing. Not even darkness. Just… emptiness. An absence of everything, as if nothing ever existed. When the warmth of the morning sun soaked into my face, I awoke with the hope that the strange void was the end of a nightmare, that I could roll over and find Henry sleeping soundly next to me. My eyes had yet to open, scared of what I'd find, but I felt the rustle of a body on the bed.

"Good morning," Aunt Mary's voice spoke, causing my heart to sink further into the chasm of my chest. "Or should I say good afternoon?"

I rolled over and pried open one eye to find her sitting next to me, my bedroom bright with a misplaced glow; the afternoon sun. A moan escaped my dry lips. "What time is it?"

"Twelve-thirty, dear," she replied and stood. I cracked open both my lids and glanced down where she had sat, where I'd laid out my clothing the night before. It was missing.

I bolted upright and pulled at the blankets around me. "Where is it?" I cried desperately. "Where is everything?"

Mary leaned over and gently grabbed my hands, holding them tightly within her own, forcing me to calm and look at her face.

"Shh, Dianna, settle yourself," she said. "Your things are fine. I came in this morning and found you curled up with them." I watched as she let me go and grabbed a neatly folded pile of items from the bedside table. "I washed everything the best I could and fixed the rip in the jacket's shoulder." She cleared her throat as she stole a glance at the outrageously large ruby pendant hanging from my neck. "And I cleaned the boots up, too."

Stunned, I accepted the fresh pile of clothes from her and hugged them tightly. "I'm sorry," I told her, "I don't know what's wrong with me."

"I think I do," she replied, and my eyes widened. How could she possibly know? "You've clearly been through something life-changing. Whether it was good or bad, that's something I may never learn. But the shock is going to sit with you for a while, dear."

I didn't know how to respond so I just nodded.

"Can you tell me *anything*?" she asked. "Did someone take you?"

I shook my head and fixated my gaze on the bed.

"Okay, did you go meet someone? Are you in some kind of trouble?"

Another slight shake.

"Dianna, you gotta give me something," Mary insisted, "I'm going crazy wondering what could have possibly happened to you for over three weeks. Should I be worried? Should I get you some help?"

"No," I managed. "I'll be fine. I just need some time." *Time in Mom's office*, I thought to myself.

"Very well." Mary stood from the bed and straightened out her knitted cardigan. "I'm going to head over to the bakery in a bit, see how Samantha's doing. You should get yourself cleaned up and head over if you can. Say hi, see if she needs anything. I think she'd like to talk to you."

"About what?"

Mary tipped her head and shot me a look.

I inhaled deeply. "Ah, she wants to buy it from me."

"You should consider it," my aunt suggested. "You were thinking of selling it, anyway. This way, it'd stay in the family."

The memory of me telling Henry all about my parent's bakery flashed across the back of my mind, and the hopeful look on his face when I wanted him to come back and run it with me. "I'll think about it."

"Good," Mary replied, "I'll see you later, then. When you're done at the bakery, come by the house for supper."

I tried to hide my rolling eyes and cast my gaze to the window. The second she left I planned on turning Mom's office upside down for a ticket back to Henry.

"And feed that poor boy downstairs, would ya?" she added as she exited my bedroom.

I couldn't suppress the groan that climbed out of my gut. I'd forgotten about John. The eager beaver, ready and waiting to help me tie my shoes and lift my spoon. But the thought quickly turned into an idea.

If he wanted to help, I knew the perfect job for him.

# CHAPTER FOUR

"**S**o, what is it exactly that I'm looking for?" John asked as he handed me another ancient parchment to add to the growing pile. He'd been so eager to help that when I asked him, he didn't even let me finish speaking. Just stopped preparing food for me and hopped on it like an obedient boy scout.

"I told you," I answered, already annoyed with him, and pointed to the chalkboard on the wall. "Anything that has those names, objects, or places on it."

The list consisted of the possible names Henry, Finn, Gus, and Charlie would have gone by, Cupers Cove before it was known as Cupid's, The Cobhams, plus the names of two ships; The Devil's Heart and The Burning Ghost. We'd found numerous things that mentioned The Cobhams, but mostly historical documents that told the earlier stories of her piracy; hide outs, conquests, her ties back to England, etc. Nothing about her whereabouts post-1707.

"Okay," John replied, still unsure, "And why are we doing this?"

I didn't even bother to look up from the document I was reading. "Because it's important that I know what happened to those people."

He opened another box and began rifling through its contents. "Are they ancestors of yours, or something?"

"You could say that."

"Those sound like pirate ship names," he continued. "Were your ancestors pirates?"

I finished another document and added it to the discard pile. "No," I shook my head, "I mean, yes. Sort of."

"So, why do you suddenly need to find out what happened to them?"

I grabbed the last box and slammed it down on the table, the force sending a bolt of pain up through my shoulder. "Jesus, John. Enough with the questions! Just help me or get out."

He coiled back, stunned, his feelings clearly hurt. I

immediately felt a tinge of regret, but I smashed it down, refusing to feel bad for the man who'd cheated on me. It may have felt like a lifetime ago, but hardly a month had passed since that fateful text came through.

"I'm sorry," he said quietly, "I'll shut up."

He turned his back to me and continued reading an old book he'd found among the mess. I just stood there and stared at him, unable to truly squashed the anger I harbored for him. There was something to be said about second chances, wasn't there? It's what my mother would have done. John was here, had been here in my absence, helping. Doing what he could. And now, here he remained, eager to make amends.

I stole a glance at the clock on the wall. "Hey, we've been at this all afternoon," I told him. "Let's take a break and head to my aunt's for supper."

He turned to face me, excited and hopeful. "Yeah?"

"Sure, why not?" I replied and grabbed my jacket, giving him a quick grin as I carefully slipped it on. "She told me to feed you, anyway."

\*\*\*

Mary was far too delighted to have us show up at her door. I sat at her massive oak table with its miss-matched chairs and fiddled with the quirky trinkets on the ledge next to me. She scuttled around the kitchen, tending to the stove, slicing some homemade bread, grabbing dishes from the cupboards.

"Here," John said and jumped up from his chair, "Let me set the table, Mary."

He grabbed the old-fashioned, amber-colored glass plates from her hands and placed them on the table before going back and fetching some silverware. He maneuvered around so comfortably, and I had to remind myself that he'd been there the whole time I was gone. He looked more at home at my aunt's than I did.

We sat around and ate seven-layer dinner until our bellies couldn't hold another bite. Mary told crude jokes and John turned red in the face from laughing at her. It didn't take long for me to melt into the comfortable scene and join in on the laughter. It was hard to be anything but happy around Mary.

"So, what did you two do all afternoon?" she asked, taking a sip of her tea.

My eyes flitted to John's, trying to warn him not to say anything, but what would he know? He had no idea the connection my aunt would make.

"We were going through stuff in Dianna's mom's office."

Mary quirked an eyebrow in my direction. "Oh?"

"Yeah," John continued, "She's trying to find something to do with her ancestors and some pirate ships."

Mary turned her full attention to me. "What exactly are you looking for, Dianna?" she asked, challenging me.

"I just wanted to know more about Mom's side of the family," I told her with a shrug. "When I was in the hospital, the doctors were prodding me with questions about my family's medical history, and I only really knew dad's. It just sparked a curiosity, that's all."

I looked at John and his brow furrowed in confusion. "Then, why are you looking back so far?" he asked. "The medical history of your three-hundred-year-old ancestors wouldn't really matter that much, would it?" then he added, "Man, would they even have records like that back then?"

I cringed and slouched down into my chair.

"No," Mary replied and sipped her tea, her accusing eyes searching my face, "they wouldn't."

John stood and began collecting the empty dishes, the silent fight between my aunt and I completely washing over his head. "Well, wouldn't matter, anyway. We didn't find what she was looking for." He turned then and headed toward the bathroom.

I found it strange that John's words seemed to make Mary relax. "Well, I still have one more box," I told her.

"And if you don't find what you're looking for?" Mary asked. A tinge of sadness in her voice.

I realized then, what she was worried about. Everything I was doing, looking through my mother's things like a madwoman, searching for something… it's exactly what my dad had been doing in his final days. Mary must have watched him descend into madness, trying to find answers, trying to find... my mother.

My eyes glossed over with tears, but I forced them down and looked away. "I don't know," I replied quietly, "But I'm not going to find it, am I?"

Mary reached across the table and took my hands in hers, giving it a gentle squeeze. "No, dear, I don't think you will. So, I suggest you make peace with whatever happened to you and move on. You have a life, Dianna. A life worth living. Your father, in those last months, that wasn't living. He was a ghost." She waited for me to answer and, when I failed, she squeezed my hand again. "Ya hear me?"

I nodded, the only answer I could afford because keeping the tears at bay was almost impossible. Aunt Mary scooted her chair over to mine and wrapped her arms around me. I laid my head against her shoulder and let go of the thin wall that held my emotions down.

"There, there," she said with a soft coo and smoothed my hair. "Let it out, m'love. It'll help you heal."

John entered the room then. "Jesus!" he squawked, "What's the matter? What happened?" He came over to my side and crouched down so he could look at my tear-stained face against Mary's shoulder. "Dianna, are you okay?"

I broke free of my aunt's embrace and leaned back in my chair, wiping my face. "Yeah, I'll be fine," I assured them both. "Just take me home."

Hesitant, he offered his hand for me to take and I slowly slipped mine into it. I felt his body relax and fill with delight at the gesture. I'm sure, to him, it seemed I was giving in, softening to his eagerness to make amends. But, really, I just wanted to go home and wallow in the privacy of my bedroom. I needed to truly mourn the loss of Henry and my family aboard The Devil's Heart, so I could move on and try to create a life for the child I held inside me.

Absentmindedly, I brushed my other hand over my belly and fought back more tears. But Mary caught it and I watched as the cogs of her brain clicked into place as she finally realized the true source of my sorrow. Our eyes caught one another, and I gave a quick, discreet shake of my head to tell her not to say anything in front of John.

He walked me to the door and bent down to grab my shoes, placing them at my feet. All the while, I couldn't tear my gaze from Aunt Mary as she stood next to the table and tried to contain her emotions. One arm wrapped tightly around her torso, her other reached up and placed a hand over her trembling mouth and her eyes glossed over with tears of joy or pity... I wasn't really sure. John opened the door for me and gave Mary a wave after saying thank you for supper. When his backed turned, she mouthed the words *'I'm sorry'* to me and I just nodded.

I know. Me, too.

\*\*\*

I awoke the next morning, groggy and dry-mouthed from crying all night. After John and I returned the night before, I headed up to my room with the last box, worried about the way it felt almost empty in my arms. I sat on my bed and lifted the cardboard lid, not surprised to find only a few random documents, most of which were just certificates of authentication for artifacts I knew were downstairs. I shoved the box aside and cried myself to sleep.

That was it. That was the last of... everything. But, the more I thought about it, the more I realized that I'd been wasting my time. My mother had spent years collecting those things, secretly looking for a way back to the past. Years later, my father had gone through it all and driven himself mad with the lack of answers it produced. Why did I think I could magically see something they didn't? But that wasn't the only question that crossed my mind as I descended the stairs to the smell of coffee brewing.

Why, so many years after my mother's death, did my dad suddenly get the idea to look? And what exactly was he searching for? Did he know my mother's time-traveling secret all those years, or did he suddenly figure it out?

I poured myself a cup of coffee and turned to the dining room to see John, tool belt around his waist, outside cutting lumber on a table saw through the giant hole in my house covered with clear poly. He straightened and turned to find me standing there and I raised my cup. He smiled and set down his stuff before coming inside.

"Good morning," he greeted and came into the kitchen.

"Morning," I replied and handed him a cup of coffee.

He graciously accepted it and nervously looked away, driving his attention to the milk jug. "Did you, uh, sleep well? After…"

I sighed and cringed inwardly. He'd heard me crying the night before. "Yeah, sorry," I said and scooped up a muffin, "I'm okay if that's what you're thinking. I just… there's a lot going on that I have to deal with emotionally."

John set his coffee down on the island and stepped closer, forcing me to tear my gaze from my cup and look at his glistening blue eyes. In them, I saw sympathy, a bit of regret, and an eagerness for redemption. I knew John truly felt sorry for cheating on me, and he's more than proved his willingness to make amends. I could easily give up my mission of returning to the past and stay here, with John. Build a life. Raise the baby as ours. I had a house and an established business to take over. We had everything needed to live a happy, comfortable life here in Newfoundland.

But would I truly be happy?

I continued to stare at the man before me, so open and ready for me to accept him back, and I knew I could be content. Someday. But would that be enough for me? I smiled and slid my hand across the island top and covered his hand with mine.

"I know you're sorry, John," I told him. "And I forgive you. I really do." He visibly relaxed, as if a great weight had been extracted from his body. "But, what about your job? What about—" I motioned to myself, "all of this? I've got some... stuff going on. Demons I'd have to put to rest. I'm not even sure I can do that, I'm not sure what I can offer you."

He took our embracing hands and held them to his chest as he moved closer to me, the familiar feeling of his beating heart pulsing heavily under my touch.

"I don't want anything from you, Dianna," he told me. "I swear. I just want to be here for you. Maybe, in time, you'll open back up to me. Maybe you won't. But I won't go anywhere, not unless you want me to." John took a deep and nervous breath as he inched even closer. "I can't believe it took you becoming a missing person for me to realize what I could lose. I never want to feel that way again. I don't want to lose you." He leaned down, then, and placed a gentle kiss on the side of my mouth.

John pulled away and released my hand from his. "I'm fixing the patio door," he told me and cleared his throat. "The window and door arrived this morning and I'm just putting in the last of the framing right now. Should be done this afternoon."

"Thank you," I replied, "Let me know how much it cost, I'll pay you back."

He waved his hand. "No need."

"No, seriously," I insisted, "Insurance will pay for it."

"Oh, sure," John replied awkwardly, "yeah that works."

"I'm going to make some breakfast," I changed the topic, attempting to cut the weird tension in the air. "Want some?"

He brightened, probably remembering how much he loved my cooking. "Yeah! That would be awesome." Happily, he scooped up his work gloves and gave me a wink before slipping out the small opening that led outside.

It didn't take long for me to settle back into the thing I loved so much; cooking. While the omelets fried on the stove, I popped some homemade bread in the toaster and then stood at the island where I could stare out at the open house before me. My eyes scanned the gorgeous interior, the built-in shelving, the gorgeous beach rock hearth that surrounded the wood stove, the weathered and slightly warped farmhouse wooden floor that touched every corner of the house.

I loved this place. So did Mom. I remembered then, a secret little nook Mom had made over by the woodstove. One of the stones came loose and she turned it into a hiding place for me to stash my beach glass.

I left the kitchen and strolled over, knowing

exactly which stone it was. My fingers grasp the edges and gave a slight tug. It resisted at first, but I could feel that it was loose, the grout surrounding it long crumbled away. With a bit of force, the stone came out, and there was my beach glass. Green, white, and brown shards softened by the tumbling waters.

As a kid, I was convinced they were jewels and Mom told me that I had to keep them safely hidden. I scooped the tiny pieces into my hand and returned the stone to its nook. Then, as I turned around to face the house, something dawned on me. Nooks and crannies. Hidden cupboards. Secret panels.

Mom loved that stuff.

The house had to be full of them. If there was something worth hiding, like the key to time travel, she'd never have kept it out in the open in her office. A new hope washed over me then and I came alive with purpose. I began frantically searching the house, every inch, every ledge, pushing on panelboard, picking at the seams of moldings, and knocking on walls.

Eventually, after finding nothing more than a few toys, more beach glass, and some old books, I planted myself on the stairs, ridden with defeat. What was I doing? Did I really want to waste my life searching for something that possibly didn't exist? Did I want to become my parents, both lost down two different roads in life?

"Dianna!" John shouted from the kitchen,

"Jesus!"

I descend the stairs into a cloud of smoke and suddenly remembered the omelets.

"Shit!" I yelled and grabbed a towel to help fan the smoke out the opening in the dining room. "I'm sorry! I was looking for something. I got distracted."

After tossing the burnt frying pan into the sink, I expected John to snap. To yell at me and tell me to get my crap together. But I was surprised when he turned, fanning the smoke, and began to laugh. "Guess we're just having toast."

I couldn't help the smile that spread to my lips and let out a laugh. Together, neither of us unable to stop laughing, we grabbed the cold toast and headed out to the front porch to sit down with our cups of coffee. I could see then how easy it would be to just... *be* with John. Memories washed over me of all the different reasons why I fell for him in the first place.

The sparkling blue eyes, his infectious laugh and the warmth that always radiated from him. John was like the center of gravity and people easily fell into a comfortable rotation around him. I let him throw an arm around my shoulders and we both sat in silence as we sipped coffee and chewed the dry toast. It was a tiny taste of what my life could be like if I ever decided to let go of the past.

Just then, a car came down the gravel road toward us and I saw that it was Aunt Mary's. She pulled to a stop and got out, waving before ducking back in to grab something. As she walked up to the front steps, I saw that it was a book.

"Good afternoon, you two," she greeted and took off her over-sized sunglasses, noting our unexpected embrace. "Dianna, dear, can I speak to you for a second?"

"Uh, sure," I replied, breaking free of John's arm and standing up. "Is everything okay?"

Mary gripped the book tight and smiled. "Yes, everything's fine. Just have something to show you."

John sensed the strange air between us and stood to meet our faces, rubbing the back of his neck nervously. "I'll head out and grab some real food."

I nodded. "Thanks."

As I watched him drive off down the old gravel, I turned to Mary. "So, what's up? What's with the book?"

Mary reached into her pocket and pulled out a large bottle of pills. "These are prenatal vitamins," she told me and handed the bottle over. "Take them, it'll give the baby all the stuff it needs."

"Thanks," I replied and motioned to the book. "What's that?"

She heaved a heavy sigh and held the old book out to me. I took it in my hands and admired the worn red leather of the cover and the intricate symbol of a sun and moon burned into the front.

"This," she started, "is your mother's journal."

My breath caught in my chest as my eyes flicked

to my aunt, daring her to tell me she was joking.

"I gave it to your father, a few years ago, thinking it would give him some closure." My aunt stopped to clear her throat. "Clearly, that was a bad idea. Whatever's contained in that book drove your father into madness."

"Then, why give it to me?"

"Because I have a feeling the words your mother wrote weren't meant for him. They were meant for you. If you can read it and, I dunno, get some answers or closure or… something. Maybe you can get over whatever happened to you and come back to us. Come back to your life. *Here*." Her emphasis on the last word caught my attention.

"Did you read this?"

Mary held her chin high. "I read a little. I saw enough to put some pieces together. I don't believe it, but it's hard to argue otherwise." I opened my mouth to try to explain, but she cut me off. "Nope. I don't want to hear it. I don't want to know. You disappeared, went… some place far away. I get that. What I want from you is something else entirely."

I shrugged and shook my head. "What?"

"Read your mother's journal," she started, "If you don't find the answers you need then promise to stop. Leave whatever happened to you behind, stop looking, stop wanting whatever it is you think you want. Stay here, fix the house, run the bakery, and raise that baby. Whether or not that life includes John is up to you." She paused, her words slowly sinking in. "Can you do that?"

I rubbed my thumb over the sun and moon on the cover, admiring that my mother's hands had put the symbols there. My mom, the time traveler. The magical woman from the past. I held the edge to my nose and inhaled deeply, surprised to find that the slightest hint of her perfume still held onto the pages, the scent brought tears to my eyes. This was my last hope. If the secret to going back to Henry even existed, it had to be in that journal. My father may have found it, but maybe he didn't know or understand it properly, the way I would.

"Yes," I told Aunt Mary, agreeing because there was a high chance I would never have to uphold my end of the bargain. I could be on my way back to Henry any day and that thought set fire to something inside of me. I held up the journal in admiration and awe. "I can do that."

# CHAPTER FIVE

After John got back with some breakfast sandwiches, I wolfed mine down and told him my pain meds were making me drowsy, so I excused myself to go upstairs. I felt horrible for lying, I was actually trying to cut down on the pain meds for fear of the effect they'd have on the baby, but I had to get away. The call of Mom's journal rang like an echo in my head and it was all I could think about. The answer I needed. The secret to time travel. My ticket back to Henry.

It could be waiting within those very pages.

I rested my back against the headboard, bent my knees, and propped the journal open on my thighs before taking a deep breath and carefully opening the pages. The image of Mom's handwriting struck me hard and I fought not to cry. I ran my fingertips over the pen scrawl, feeling the indent from the pressure put on the pen, imagining her writing the words. Surprisingly, her first entry wasn't long before my birth.

*Jan. 7th 1990*

*Martha was right. Oh, Lord, was she ever right. I can hear her now, cursing my name, probably regretting the years she spent raising me. All those times I refused to heed her warnings about time, I never understood the repercussions until now. But, here I am, lost and stranded in the future, with no way back. I thank the gods that time saw fit to keep me home in Newfoundland, but it is a Newfoundland I do not know.*

*I've found refuge in the church, a place that, thankfully, still exists in this time. It has been three months since I washed ashore and was found by Mr. Abbott, the local minister who leads the church. I pretended to have no memory of who I am or where I came from. They made me speak to law officials called policemen, and they've failed at tracking down my origin, of course.*

*So, I've been left here to work for the church that gives me lodging and I've befriended the museum curator, a person who collects information and artifacts from our land's history. I figure it the best place to find my way home.*

*Only time shall tell.*

*Constance Cobham*

I flipped to the next entry as I digested the words I'd just read. Mom found herself lost in time roughly a year before I was born. Which meant, she'd met my father not long after she arrived. The next few entries were much the same as the first; Mom documenting every attempt she made at getting back home, and how every single one failed.

She listed all the different things she tried, relics she'd found through the museum, but nothing that was of any use. Nothing that gave me the answer. I could tell, after the fourth entry, how frustrated she was getting. Some words were blurred from drops of water that had soaked in and bled the ink, but I quickly realized they were most likely tears. How scared she must have been, lost in a future she couldn't comprehend.

For me, going back in time was scary, but it was a time I knew, a place I could easily digest from reading books, growing up here and knowing some of the histories of Newfoundland. I saw things and knew what they were. But Mom... she would have had no idea how to process things like cars, and cities, and technology.

*Feb. 14th, 1990*

*It has been four months and eight days since I washed ashore in this future Newfoundland. I thought I would have found a way back by now, but I'm beginning to think my efforts are wasted. Everything fails, and nothing seems to bring me closer to an answer.*

*But today I met a man. A handsome and kind man named Arthur Sheppard. It appears that this day is what they call Valentine's, a time of year people celebrate their love for one another. He ventured into the museum gift shop in search of a present for his sister, Mary. We talked for hours, and I'm quite fond of him. He invited me over to his home for supper tonight.*

*Perhaps this future Newfoundland won't be so bad after all. I know I must find a way back home, eventually, to correct the threads of time. I don't belong here. But, perhaps, I could dabble in a little romance while I wait. What could it hurt?*

*Constance*


I closed the journal to let out a deep breath, it felt like I'd been holding it in the whole time. Mom's story mirrored my own in so many ways. She found herself lost in another time, scared, stranded. Then found a man who made her happy, not realizing how she could fall deeply and dangerously in love like I had with Henry. Still, as sweet as it was to see my parents meet through my mother's eyes... I'd yet to find what I truly wanted. Hesitantly, I continued reading.

The further I read, the further apart the entry dates became. It appeared that Mom had been distracted from her mission of returning home, distracted by the love she felt for Dad. Through my mother's eyes, I saw how they both fell in love, bought our house, and then, finally, discovered the news they were pregnant with me.

*June 2nd, 1991*

*I can feel the child growing inside me, and my belly is beginning to show signs of change. I'm constantly tormented by guilt. I should be searching for a way home but I'm here, in the future, enthralled with the wonderful life I've fallen into. I fear that if I found a way back now, while pregnant, I'd retreat further into a shell of despair. I cannot do that to Arthur, my love, the most wonderful man to ever grace this Earth. I must set aside my mission until the baby is born. If I'm to break Arthur's heart someday, I'd like to know he and our child will have one another to love.*

*Constance*

Knowing my mother truly loved my dad reassured me in a way I didn't realize I needed until then. Through all of this, I wondered and worried about her feelings for him. Now I felt bad that I ever doubted her. My shoulder began to throb, so I laid down to take the weight off, refusing to pop any more pain meds. With my good arm, I held up the journal and continued reading. When I saw the date, my stomach fluttered with an unsettling emotion, a strange mix of fear and excitement. The date read the second day in December.

My birthday.

*Dec. 2nd, 1991*

*Time is passing at a rate I cannot fathom, and each day brings me closer to Dianna's birth. I'd told myself I would set aside my formidable mission of getting home, but I'm weak. I'm also worried. I've spent far too much time in this era, and I fear what my presence has done to alter the threads of time. Nevertheless, part of me doesn't care. Some days I tell myself that I'll just abandon my quest and stay here, with Arthur, with Dianna. I'm happy. I'm loved.*

*I write this as I sit in my new home office and stare out the window, admiring the reflections on the twilight water, and remembering the night I came here. It feels like such a long time ago.*

And that was it. That particular entry seemed to drop off. As if Mom had been interrupted and couldn't finish it. Desperately, I turned the page, eager to find out what happened.

*Dec. 3rd, 1991*

*I'm able to steal a few precious moments to log this entry, I feel it's important I do so. Two life-*

*changing events happened in the course of 24 hours. First, Dianna, my sweet and beautiful girl, was born late last night. I'm completely and utterly drowning in an obsession with her perfection. I never knew love could be this way, to take on a form such as this. I can't imagine ever not loving her. She's resting soundly in the bassinet next to my bed, a sleeping Arthur by my side, as I write this.*

*The second notable event is that I found it. I know how to get back. The problem I now face is that I can't bring myself to do it. I cannot leave them. They are my world, and I theirs.*

*What a bittersweet feeling it is.*

*Constance.*


My heart beat wildly as I turned the page, searching for more. She wouldn't have done that, would she? After everything, to discover the way back, and not write it down? Page after page, I grew more frantic. All that proceeded that last entry was a collection of my childhood pieced together through my mother's adoring eyes. Every birthday, every scrape and bruise, major milestones, locks of my hair, handprints, everything. Her private journal had morphed into my baby book. Mom truly did leave behind her life in favor of the one she'd built in the future.

I let out a fierce scream and chucked the journal across the room where it smashed into a wall and fell to the floor. My stomach dropped when I heard John's footsteps running up the stairs and down the hall toward my room. He swung open the door and blew in, eyes wide with panic.

"Jesus, Dianna, are you alright?" he asked and sprinted over to the bed where I sat, crying into my hands.

"No!" I yelled, tears and snot bubbling down my face. "No, I'm not alright. It's *over*, it's all over. I'm *stuck* here."

John's shoulders relaxed as he heaved a sigh and sat down. "Look, I'm not going to pretend I don't see that something's going on. And I don't expect you to tell me." He quirked a smile. "Heck, I'm just thankful that you've let me stay here at all. But I just want you to know that I'm here for whatever you need. Friendship or more than friendship, it's up to you. I just... I love you, Dianna. I want you to know that."

My lips pursed as I contemplated telling him everything. But I knew, deep down, he'd never be able to accept it. He'd always wonder if the woman he loved was some kind of crazy. And maybe I was. It certainly felt that way. But I had to give him something, let him in. He earned that much.

"John," I croaked, "I'm pregnant."

I watched his face changed and his big blue eyes light up with pure delight before I realized what was running through his mind.

"It's not yours," I broke it to him, "It's—" I didn't know how to shape the words. "I met someone while I was gone."

"Oh," he replied, the disappointment radiating

from him. "That's... I guess that's fair. It's not like we were together." He seemed to be collecting his thoughts and feelings about the breaking news. Surprisingly, I worried that it would drive him away. I actually didn't want John to leave. Not yet, anyway. Not until I figured out my feelings. "What do you need?" he asked.

"Need?"

John took my hand. "Yes, what do you need? What do you want? Should I go back to Alberta? Because I will if that would make you happy. Or should I stay? D-do you want me to help raise that baby?" His own words seemed to overwhelm him, but he still smiled in determination.

"Oh, God, no. John, I could never ask you to do that," I told him.

"Then ask me something, for the lov'a God," he replied in desperation. "I feel useless here. Give me something to do other than pacing the floors, listening if you're okay."

My heart ached for him. I wasn't sure what I could promise John for a future. Heck, even a present. I could only live a minute from minute as I faced my new reality that Henry was gone forever. I'd never get back to the people I loved so dearly. But I had a responsibility to the life inside of me. Hesitantly, I pulled John's hand toward me.

"Just lay with me?" I asked and scooted over to make room for him. He didn't think twice as he moved and lay down next to me in my sunlit bedroom. His arm came up to hold me in a gentle, respectful embrace and we soon fell asleep to the soothing sounds of our own breathing.

***

The next day I awoke with a sliver of purpose. I had decided that if I were to truly put the past to rest, I had to get rid of everything. The museum still waited for most of Mom's belongings and collections, so I already had a home for a lot of it. I spent the day packing and cleaning and labeling. It hurt a little, to see Mom's office so empty. But I told myself that I was making room for a new beginning. It was now my office, to use it as I saw fit. Maybe I'd take over the bakery after all. Or maybe I'd sell it and use the money to open a small restaurant.

It had been a few days now since I checked out of the hospital in St. John's and the stitches in my shoulder were healing nicely. I removed the old dressing and cleaned the wound before attaching a new, fresh one. The sky was turning pink as the sun prepared to set and I carried one last box out to the dining room. This was a special box, one I had set aside to store my own personal things in. Maria's jacket, Henry's necklace, my clothing from Nathaniel, most of the items I'd first discovered in that fateful chest, and some other small trinkets that I couldn't part with but also knew had to be put out of sight.

Like Mom's journal.

I stood at the dining room table, the same way I did on that momentous night and stared out at the vast ocean as I stacked everything neatly inside the box. Mom's journal was the last to go, it sat on the table next to the box. I scooped it up, rubbing my fingers over the sun and moon on the cover once again and, for the last time, recalled the new memories I now had of my mother. She had been a bright light in my life, and I felt closer to her now because I knew her secret. The secret we now both shared. I brushed a hand across my belly and smiled.

"Don't worry, little one," I spoke quietly, "I'll be the best mom I can be. I promise to tell you stories of adventure and magic. How the ocean can grant wishes—"

Suddenly, as I looked at the journal once again, my blood ran hot with an idea. A realization. Frantically, I searched for the entry, the day of my birth. I spread the book out on the table when I reached the page and read it again. Mom had been interrupted, probably because she had gone into labor with me. But what if it were something else entirely? In her next entry, I'm born, and she admits that she'd found the way back. So, what happened between those two entries?

I flipped to the cover again, noting the hand burned sun and moon, and then cast my gaze out to the colorful ocean that waited just outside my door. Then, out of nowhere, Mom's voice came to life in my ears.

*"If you were to sail out there, to the water, and meet the moon and the sun in the waves at just the right time, they'd grant you a wish."*

My breathing quickened past the point of control as the lightbulb exploded in my brain. That was it. That was the answer I'd been searching for. Mom *did* find a way back. And, in a way, she *did* document it. She told me that fable and then burned the symbols into her journal. I recalled the entry when Mom must have found it, how she noted standing in her new office, staring out at the water. It *had* to be it.

I had all of my belongings right there in a box in front of me. John was gone into town to pick up supper. The sun and moon were reflecting on the ocean's waves. The timing was perfect. As if the universe aligned to show me the way. I bolted for the kitchen to grab a pen and paper, feverishly jotting down some parting words to leave behind.

*John and Mary,*

*Thank you for everything. Really. I don't know what I would have done without both of you in my life. John, I want you to know that I really do forgive you. You're an amazing man, friend, and partner. If things were different, I have no doubt in my mind that we'd be together. But, I want you to find someone who will make you happy. Thank you for being here and helping me heal.*

*Mary, you have always been the shining light in*

*my life post-Mom. You turned me into the woman I am today. Thank you for everything. Take care of the house and tell Samantha she can have the bakery.*

*If you're reading this, it means I succeeded where Dad had failed, and I'll be long gone. Maybe I'll return one day, maybe I won't. Only time will tell.*

*All my love,*
*Dianna*

I left the notebook open to my letter on the kitchen counter and ran upstairs to grab my old leather shoulder bag. I stuffed a few clean pairs of underwear inside, plus a Diva Cup, deodorant, and my toothbrush. I descended the stairs two at a time and scuttled around the house, scooping up things I knew I'd need this time around and stuffing them in the satchel.

A bag of schillings from Mom's collection, a large dagger, my prenatal vitamins, a lighter, a bottle of rubbing alcohol, my pain meds and antibiotics, and a full water canister. I would be the most prepared time traveler who ever existed.

Then I went back to the dining room and removed my clothes before slipping back into the garments I'd brought here with me. My adopted red jacket fit like a glove and I noted the immaculate job Mary had done at mending the tear. My wounded shoulder protested as I lifted the satchel and slipped my head through. The bag hung heavily at my side, but I tossed Mom's journal in, along with some snacks and tightened the convenient drawstring before locking the giant metal clasp in place. I stopped for a moment to look around and took a deep breath.

Lastly, I scooped up my ruby necklace and looped it over my head. "I'm coming home, Henry."

John would be back soon and my window of opportunity to get far enough out on the water was closing by the second. I ran outside and down to the water's edge where our old motorboat was and shoved it into the water before clumsily hopping in. It took a few labored tries, but I yanked on the pull start a fourth time and the motor roared to life.

"Yes!" I shouted to the skies above. I hit the gas and maneuvered the tiny vessel out to the moon's reflection on the waves, the pink highlight of the setting sun nearly gone. I worried that I was too late but leaned over the side and dipped my hand in the cool water.

"Please," I begged the universe, "Take me back to Henry." I waited a few seconds and when nothing happened, I asked again. "I wish to be taken back to Henry, please!"

Still nothing.

I released my hold on the boat's edge and sat on the damp bottom, defeated, fighting back the wave of anger I felt building up. That was it. My last shot. And it didn't even work. I felt like a fool and panicked as I thought of John discovering the letter

I left behind. I was about to turn the boat around when something caught my eye, a movement in the practically still water just a few feet from the side of my tiny vessel.

I moved closer to the front where I could get a better look and scanned the ocean's surface. What light lingered from the sun had gone and all that remained was moonlight and pure darkness, but I could see, in the reflection of the moon, the hint of ripples fading out from the center of... something. I inched closer, straining my eyes to see when something emerged from the water and splashed my face. I fell on my ass and scrambled back to my knees to see what it was, but the darkness shrouded everything.

"Hello," a strange sound voiced, eliciting a yelp from me. I still couldn't actually see anything.

Or anyone.

"Hi," I replied, "w-who's there?" The boat rocked and tilted to the side as I braced the edges of the wooden bench seat. Then, as the boat drifted further into a ray of moonlight, a figure manifested from the water. No, the shape... itmanifested *of* water. I screamed and backed away.

"You summon my help and then scream in my presence?" the water-being stated. Only, it's voice, it didn't quite come from the shape. The echoing sound seemed to come from the water all around as if the ocean itself had spoken to me. But I continued to stare, digesting what my eyes were seeing. It mimicked a human form but was made entirely of water. I could see the lapping waves and the pale moonlight behind it as if peering through a window on a rainy night.

"I'm sorry," I told it, mouth gaping, "you just startled me. I've never seen anything like you before."

The thing pushed itself up and leaned further into my boat. "I'm a siren of the ocean," it said. "If you do not know what I am, then how did you know to summon me?"

I thought for a moment. Mom must have recalled the fable from her own childhood memories. In her journal, she'd mentioned being raised by Martha, the Celtic witch. Who knew the plethora of magical knowledge she subconsciously harbored in that brain of hers? "My mother," I replied, "she knew a little about magic. She told me about the wish when I was a child."

"Be that as it may," the siren spoke with a warning, "what you seek goes against the laws of time. You cannot go back unless you are from the past."

"But I've done it before," I replied desperately.

The creature appeared surprised as it accepted my words. "Curious."

"What's curious?"

"I've roamed the seas for millennia, and I've only known one thing to overpower the laws of time," the siren told me, and its face appeared to morph with the shape of a grin as it cocked its head to the side.

My patience grew thin and I worried someone would spot me out on the water.

"And? What was it?"

The creature pushed even further into my little boat and brought its face close to mine. I could smell the saltwater and feel the cool sea breeze that flowed around its shape. "Fate." It drew back again, the shape of a smile still molded into its face. "It appears someone's heart calls to you from the past, dearie."

Before I could reply, the creature lunged backward and leaped into the sea with a heavy splash, soaking me and covering the bottom of the boat with water. As I wiped the wetness from my face, I peered out to where it had disappeared and spotted a tiny swirling movement on the surface. It grew larger, faster, and before I could prepare myself, the tiny swirl had morphed into a massive whirlpool. The mouth opened even further, and the moving force sucked my boat into a rotation around the perimeter as I grabbed ahold of the sides, bracing for what was to come. The whipping current grabbed hold of the boat and knocked me around inside it. I fought to hold on, to keep the craft afloat, but as I swirled down closer to the dark center, I lost control and just let go, letting the ocean and the threads of time take me once again.

# CHAPTER SIX

The familiar misty breeze of the ocean tousled my hair and stirred me from unconsciousness. I pried open my dry, sand coated mouth and rolled over to face the warm sun above, noting a couple of seagulls circling above. A coarse moan escaped my lips as I pushed my body upright to look around and found that I wasn't alone.

A stray goat sniffed at my face and let out a loud *baaaaa*, kicking my heart awake before running off. My eyes followed the animal and saw that I appeared to be on a beach with a long stretch of grass behind me, the faint hint of smoke tops in the distance.

I made it.

After assessing my body to confirm that I was okay, and still had my trusty satchel of goodies, I scrambled to my feet. Adrenaline was hot through my veins as I jumped up and down with my arms high in the air. "Yes!" I screamed to the skies and my wounded shoulder angrily protested. "I did it!"

After allowing a quick happy dance on the sand, I checked my shoulder to make sure it was alright and headed off in the direction of the smokestacks. I had to figure out where I was and find a place to stay while I sussed out the word on land. It didn't take long to find a gravel road which led into the nearby community. The landscape was familiar, but I could have been anywhere in Newfoundland for all I knew. The gravel crunched beneath the soles of my leather boots as I walked and inhaled the sweet air. I smiled as the rooftops of the town came into full view and I ran toward the small wooden sign at the end of the road.

"Harbour Grace?" I spoke out loud and then laughed to myself. I had landed where the most notorious pirate of all time, Peter Easton, fortified his base and ruled Newfoundland hundreds of years ago. History said that no ship passed through the harbor without Easton's crew claiming it. Thankfully, his reign over the area ended in the

1600s, nearly a hundred years from the past I then stood in. But that wasn't the only good thing. Harbour Grace wasn't that far from Cupers Cove, so finding out what happened to The Devil's Heart should prove to be an easy task.

My tired legs strolled along as I took in the quaint houses and bustling seaside town. The docks were alive with fishermen, merchants, traders, and the harbor was riddled with vessels of all sizes. The sight of the sails stirred something in my soul, a familiar sense of home, and I longed to be on the sea again. The smell of the sea mixed with baked goods filled my nostrils and tickled my stomach, alerting me to the fact that I was starving. I came across a tavern, the hand-painted sign telling me it was called The Slippery Cod and entered with a grin.

Inside, I found a few tables along the front window where some fishermen sat, and a weathered front desk area that looked like it doubled as a bar. "Hello?" I called. I could feel the men's eyes on me. From the swinging saloon-style doors behind the bar, a young woman came charging out with a tray full of plates and mugs, her plain cotton dress visibly worn with the days duties. She caught the sight of me and smiled.

"I'll be right with you," she told me quickly as she passed, heading toward the sitting men. I watched her set down the tray and place food and drinks in front of each eagerly awaiting man. A couple of them sized up her behind as she leaned across the table, something I'm sure she was used to but still made me sick to witness. She scooped up her empty tray and turned to come toward me when one of the men grabbed her hand and pulled her back.

"When are ye gonna sell me that boat of yers?" he asked her.

The barmaid plastered on a smile. "Now, Fergus, you know I can't part with it. I've told you a hundred times." She attempted to leave again, but the Fergus character wouldn't have it. His expression turned sour as he yanked on her arm again.

"Now ye listen here," he warned her as she wriggled against his hold. "A boat like that is nothin' for a fine young lady to have. Best sell it to a man who can use it."

I'd had enough. The era be damned, I wasn't going to stand there while a woman got harassed by a gross old man. I strolled over to them, removing my dagger from my satchel as I did, and then brought it down on the tabletop with a quick jab, the tip driving into the surface. The three men threw themselves back in their chairs and eyed the dagger with fear before turning their gazes to me. One man jumped up from his seat while pointing at my knife.

"T-that be the mark of The Burning Ghost," he announced.

I stole a quick look at my knife, knowing it once belonged to Maria but never noticed the etched skull inside a flame on the opposite side of her carved initials. I tried to hide my surprise and used this to my benefit while grinning at the shell-shocked men.

"Gentlemen," I addressed, "Do we have a problem here?"

They tipped their flat hats and scuttled around as they grabbed their coats. "No, ma'am," one replied before they all ran out the door.

I leaned forward and fetched my dagger from the table, internally reeling from what I just did, and finally sheathed it at my side instead of tossing it back in the bag. I then turned my attention to the barmaid who stood with her hands on her hips.

"Who the hell are you?" she asked, eyes wild.

"I'm—" who was I? "not from around here. I just got to town." The bard maid nodded curiously. "I'm looking for a room for a few nights. If you have one."

I noted her looking at my ears and then remembered that I forgot to take out my diamond studs, a birthday gift from my father so many years ago. Here, in this era, diamond anything would be pretty much unheard of. Jewels fit for royalty. I self-consciously pawed at my straggly hair, hoping to cover my earlobes.

She continued to eye me curiously and turned to head behind the old wooden counter. "Well, Not From Around Here, I do happen to have a couple of rooms available." She fetched a key that hung from the back wall amongst the jars of rum and handed it to me. "It's nothing fancy, but there are fresh quilts and a wash pan."

I smiled. "Thanks." An awkward silence hung between us as I wondered if I could just head to my room. "Those men, do they always harass you about your boat?"

Her eyes flashed with something and I watched her put up a wall. "Yes," she replied. "It's just a small thing my pop left to my daddy. Now it's mine." She nervously began to wipe down the bar top. "Just a tiny fishing boat, really." Then she pointed to the stairs. "Your room is at the top, first on the right."

I retreated to my room, a modest space with a single bed and a dresser with a wash pan on top. I collapsed on the bed and let it really sink in that I was there. I'd traveled back in time twice. I had a long road ahead of me to figure out what happened to The Devil's Heart, but I was on the right track. I could feel it. If I could get this far on my own, then there was nothing that would stop me. My fingers reached down into my shirt and pulled out the ruby necklace. I loved the feeling of the cold stone warming in my palm as I held it tightly.

"I'm going to find you, Henry." Absentmindedly, I rubbed my stomach with my free hand and smiled. "*We're* going to find you."

I then removed my heavy satchel and placed it on the bed in front of me. Without a second thought, I took out my diamond studs and tucked them into a tiny inside pocket for safekeeping. Then I popped a prenatal vitamin and took a swig from my canister before laying back against the pillow. Without realizing, I dozed off and woke up sometime later, the setting sun casting a purple glow across the room as a knock at my door pulled me from my sleep. I rolled off the bed and opened the door to find the barmaid.

"Apologies," she said, "I wasn't aware you were sleeping."

I rubbed my tired eyes. I had jetlag from hell. "No, it's okay," I assured her. "I have things to do, anyway."

"Well, just wanted to let you know that supper's being served in a few moments if you're hungry."

"Thanks," I replied with a yawn, "I'm starved, actually." The young woman lingered, and I could sense the tension radiating from her. "Is there anything else?"

With arms crossed over her chest, she chewed her lip before deciding to speak. "Are you truly from The Burning Ghost?"

"What?"

"Your dagger," she continued, "It bears the mark of The Burning Ghost. Everyone thought that ship was long gone. Then it recently resurfaced, causin' trouble everywhere." She stopped and let her words stew with me. "I don't want any trouble here."

I inhaled deeply. "No, I promise you, I'm not from The Cobham's ship." The relief that washed over her body was hard to ignore. "I'm here to find some friends of mine. We—" I wondered how much information I could trust this woman with. "We got separated about a week ago."

"Very good, then," the woman accepted my words, "If you're lookin' for anyone, just ask around the tavern downstairs around mealtime. All the fishermen and merchants come in for some grub, one of them should know somethin'." She turned to leave but paused at the top of the stairs. "I'm Lottie, by the way."

"It's nice to meet you, Lottie," I genuinely told her, my mind racing to think of a name I could use. Then I grinned. "I'm Dianna. Dianna White."

\*\*\*

After I cleaned myself up and changed the dressing on my shoulder, I headed downstairs to the tavern for some food with the intent to gain information about The Devil's Heart. I found the place full, bustling with chatty fishermen and locals. A few gave me a smile and a hat tip but ignored me beyond that. I found an empty chair at the end of the bar and took a seat. Before long, Lottie came charging out through the swinging doors with a heavy food tray in hand. She spotted me and, after she served a couple of patrons, came over to me from behind the bar.

"What can I get for you?" she asked as her cloth wiped the wooden surface in front of me.

I shrugged. "What do you have?"

"Well, you have a choice between a fish stew and fish stew," Lottie replied jokingly without a smile. Her humor surprised me, and I laughed as she threw me a wink. "I'll bring you somethin' to drink, as well."

I nodded. "Thanks."

While I waited, I opened my ears to the conversations around me to see if I could pick up on anything that may help my mission. I couldn't just stroll up to a stranger and ask if they've heard of The Devil's Heart. I had to be sneaky about it. Drawing too much attention to myself probably wasn't a good idea, and I was certain word had already spread about the crazy lady at the tavern with Maria Cobham's dagger.

All around, I could hear the raspy voices of fishermen mixing with the cheery tones of the locals, every person just happy to be there and relaxing with friends around good food and the warmth of the big stone fireplace near the back. As the sun set, the tavern dimmed to the glow of oil lamps that hung from the walls and anchored the center of every table.

While eating the surprisingly delicious fish stew Lottie brought me, I attempted to strike up casual chit-chat with a few sailors that sidled up to me. But, one after another, they left when I turned the conversation to The Devil's Heart. I couldn't tell if they were scared or just plain hiding something. Either way, no one would give me any helpful information. But the word must have made its way through the bustling tavern because, over the sudden sound of a fiddle filling the space, I picked up on the mention of Cupers Cove and two men planning a trip to see The Devil's Heart. My own heart skipped a beat and I turned on my stool to face the pair of sailors sitting at the table behind me.

"Gentlemen," I greeted, and they gave me a smile. "What's this I hear about a trip to Cupers Cove?"

They both exchanged a look and held their smiles. "Yes, ma'am," one replied and tipped the brim of his flat hat. "We're headin' out tomorrow morning."

"Do you have room for one more?" I asked, hopeful.

They exchanged another look, but their smiles began to fade. "Not really," the other told me. "We got some business to tend to."

The other one piped in then. "And the sea is no place for a lady, anyway."

I hopped down from my stool and took a few steps to their little table. "Lookie here," I began and narrowed my eyes. "I know you're going to see The Devil's Heart. I heard you. That's *my* ship. Those are *my* men. And I'd very much appreciate a ride home if you'd be so kind." I stood straight and tried my best to hold a firm expression, but I was dying on the inside. If these men wouldn't take me, I'd resort to smuggling myself aboard their ship if I had to.

But, rather than the off-put, angry tone I expected in reply, their expressions turned solemn. "Oh, Miss," the first man spoke. "Where have you been?"

I tried to feign confusion but that long-forgotten feeling of an anvil hitting the bottom of my stomach nearly knocked me over. Their long faces told me bad news. "What do you mean?"

"The Devil's Heart sits at the bottom of the harbour," he answered.

My breathing quickened, and I wrestled with myself not to jump across the table and force the answers from his throat. I flexed my fingers before they balled themselves into tension-filled fists.

"What happened?" I asked through gritted teeth and, when they appeared confused, I asked again, louder. "What *happened*?"

Just as I was about to grab his shoulders and scream at the poor man for not telling me, a hand locked onto my arm and hauled me off toward the stairs. Lottie dragged me through the tavern to a backroom that was tucked behind and under the old wooden staircase and pushed me up against a wall.

"I thought you said you didn't have anything to do with The Burning Ghost?" she angrily accused.

"I-I didn't," I replied. "I mean, I don't."

"Then what are you doing asking about The Devil's Heart?"

"That's my ship," I told her honestly. "I got

separated from my crew about a week or so ago and now I'm trying to find them."

"You," Lottie scoffed, eyes wide, "a woman? Part of a crew? And the Devil's crew, to boot?"

I straightened my coat and held my chin high. "Yeah, so? What's so hard to believe about that?"

"A woman is a bad omen on the sea," the barmaid explained and then smirked. "Unless her heaving breast adorns the bow."

My cheeks flushed with anger. "I'll have you know that Captain Barrett and I were to be wed," I half-lied. Truthfully, I never did accept Henry's proposal. But I would have. *I will*, I added to myself. "Those men are my family. I'm just trying to get back to them."

Lottie appeared confused and scanned my face for dishonesty. "But—" she shook her head, "I don't get it. Where have ya been? How do you not know?"

The anvil felt heavier and cold as ice as my stomach clenched tightly. "Know what?"

"Dianna," she said, her voice suddenly soft, low, weighed down with pity. "The Devil's Heart is gone." Lottie took my hand in hers as my other grabbed at my chest, tears welling in my eyes. "And so is the crew. All of them. Singed to ash and sitting at the bottom of the harbour. Those men are probably going out there to see what they can scavenge from the ship."

The tears rose and poured out over my bottom lids, cascading down my face. My mouth opened to ask what I already knew the answer to. "W-who did it?"

Lottie's hand tightened around mine and her head tilted to one side. "The Burning Ghost."

# CHAPTER SEVEN

I had left a stunned Lottie downstairs as I retreated to my room. My emotions were holding on by a thread as I struggled to stick the old brass key in the hole. When I finally got in, I slammed the door and collapsed on the bed where the thin holds gave way and my emotions tore through. I let out a long wail of pain as my heart grieved for the loss all over again. Only, this time, it was worse. At least I'd had hope before, the small sliver of hope that Henry and the crew were at least alive. I'd been taken away from them, but at least they were alive.

Or so I'd thought.

Now, I'd found my way back to the past and I was

stranded with nothing, no one to call my own. The cries were painful as they erupted from my body and I curled over in a ball to try and console myself, rocking back and forth, my arms wrapped tightly around my torso. But it didn't work. I had to exorcise the pain from my body because I was too weak to hold on to it.

All night I stayed like that, crumpled up in a sobbing ball on the bed. I had no idea how long it took me to fall asleep, but I finally did at some point. I awoke to a pounding on the door and the blinding, early morning sun. With great force, I peeled myself from the bed, realizing that I hadn't even bothered to get under the blankets, and stumbled to the door. It opened with a loud creak and Lottie stood there with a tray of food.

"Let me in," she insisted, face stern.

"Excuse me?"

The barmaid rolled her eyes and entered the room, ducking under my arm that held the door. I shut the door and returned to my bed where I sat and cuddled a pillow to my chest. I watched as Lottie scanned the room, slowly taking in my scarce belongings before walking over and setting the tray down on the bed next to me.

"You didn't come down for breakfast," she began. "And, after your breakdown—"

"It wasn't a breakdown," I snipped.

She pursed her lips and just stared at me.

"Fine," I gave in, "It was a slight breakdown, but you don't know what happened."

Lottie smirked and turned her gaze to the window. "It appears that you don't, either." She then grabbed a date from the tray and pinched it between her fingers before tossing it in her mouth. "So, I'm willing to bet I know a bit more than you do."

I shook my head, confused. "Okay, what do you want?"

She appeared offended. "Nothing."

I cocked my head to the side.

"I truly want nothing from you, Dianna," she insisted. "I'm just curious, is all. You show up here, you have ties to one of the most notorious ships around, yet... you know nothing of the recent events. Where have you been? What are you really doing here?"

"I already told you," I choked out in a whisper and gripped the pillow tighter. "The Devil's Heart was my ship, my home. We had been spending some time in Cupers Cove when we were attacked by The Cobhams." I stopped to suck in a deep breath. "I-I was taken away against my will. I only just found my way back." It was the closest to the truth I could divulge.

Lottie turned quiet as she seemed to digest my words. I picked at a piece of plain toast and sipped the tea she'd brought me while a strange, but comfortable silence hung in the air around us. I could hear the crashing of the waves not too far from the tavern, the bustling town roaming the streets and docks just outside the window and then looked her in the eye.

"Can you tell me more about what happened?" I asked Lottie.

She shrugged. "It's hard to know what's rumor and what's true," she began, "but I'd heard that The Cobhams seized the ship, tied the crew up, and set it ablaze."

"No survivors?"

Her head hung as she diverted attention to the hem of her dirty apron. "No, none that I know of."

"And people are going to the site to scavenge the ship?"

"Yes," Lottie replied. "Apparently, The Cobhams took nothing, that it was an act of revenge. So, whatever treasure may have been aboard..."

I nodded and leaned back against the headboard. "Would still be there."

I thought about the crew, tied together and left for dead as the ship burned around them. They must have been wishing for it to hurry up and sink, to stop the flames. The sound of their screams came to life in my mind. A lump formed in my throat and I forced it down. I couldn't afford another breakdown, not in front of Lottie.

"So, what's your story?"

She appeared confused. "What do you mean?"

"Who are you? Where are you from? How long have you worked at The Slippery Cod?" Lottie remained puzzled and I rolled my eyes. "Just distract me, please."

"Oh," she replied with a nod. "Well, I don't have

much of a story. I grew up here in Harbour Grace. My father was a sailor. My parents are now dead. I'm not married. And I run this tavern for my uncle while he travels abroad." She chewed on her bottom lip. "My life is quite dull, actually. I despise it. It's terribly lonely."

"I know the feeling," I blurted out. But I immediately regretted it. Lonely. That's what I would forever be if I remained there in the past. But I had no sure way back to the future. I was stuck in limbo.

"Y'know," Lottie began, "you could stay here."

A surprising smile found its way to my face. "What do you mean?"

"Here, in the tavern. I could rent you a room, long-term. Lord knows I could use the help around here, too." She swallowed hard. "And the company."

I was touched. But I could never accept. I had to find a way back to the future, there was nothing there in the past for me. But I couldn't leave just yet. Not without putting the men I love properly to rest. "Thank you. I'll… think about it."

Lottie stood, straightened out her apron and poured me some more tea. "Well, you're welcome to stay here as long as you need." She walked toward the door but paused before leaving, seeming to have more to say but decided against it and shut the door behind her.

\*\*\*

A short while later, I found myself wandering the beach, staring out at the sea. My feet took careful steps along the rocky shore as I wrapped my coat tightly across my torso and the cool misty air caressed my face. I felt lost. Not only in time, but in life. Henry was gone. Admitting those three words sent a pain unlike anything I'd ever experienced just searing through my body like a hot knife slicing into my flesh. I repeated it over and over in my mind, trying to make sense of it, willing my broken heart to believe it. Now, I was faced with a choice to stay or go home. I wondered if the sea would grant me another wish or if I were just lucky enough to get the one that was given to me. But I had asked to be taken back to Henry. I guess the laws of magic didn't care whether he was alive or not.

But it mattered to me.

There was no place for me there in 1707 without Henry. I couldn't possibly build a life for myself and our child there. At least back home I'd have Aunt Mary. I'd have a house. The answer seemed so simple. Go back. But why did I struggle to accept it?

I did have one thing to do before I left. I had to find a place and bury the necklace Henry gave me. A final resting place for my beloved, for the man who took me prisoner and stole my heart, but gave me his in return. He deserved more than a watery grave at the bottom of the harbour. I pulled it up from inside my shirt and held the heavy ruby pendant on my palm, my other hand lovingly caressing my stomach.

"We'll say goodbye to Daddy," I told the baby, "And then we'll go back home. We'll find a way." I sat down on a large, wet rock, the water soaking into my pants. But I didn't care. "One day, I'll tell you all about my adventure and how I found your father. I'll tell you what he was like, and how much he would have loved you." I inhaled deeply, fighting back tears. "God, he would have loved you fiercely."

I could feel the pain and sorrow sitting heavily in my stomach, just waiting to be released. I let it out, let it seep from my body with a stream of loud wailing and cries toward the sea. I was heartbroken, but I was angry. Angry at the universe for letting me come back to an empty life. Angry at The Cobhams for taking everything from me, and that their vile blood flowed in my veins.

I hated myself for it. So, I let it all out right there. I screamed until my throat became raw and my eyes burned dry. The ocean brought me there, and it would endure my pain. It would take it all. A pinkish-orange glow dimmed the sky before I peeled myself off that rock and headed back to The Slippery Cod.

I opened the heavy front door and entered the quiet tavern, the supper rush had yet to begin. It felt as empty as I did on the inside, the only sounds were that of my footsteps echoing off the walls around me. I wanted to retreat to the privacy of my room before the locals started to pour in, but Lottie emerged from the back-kitchen area.

"Christ, where have you been?" she asked me, a sense of urgency in her tone.

I hugged myself tightly, hoping the evidence of my emotional purge wasn't too clear on my face. "I went for a walk," I told her. "Why, what's wrong?"

She reached into the front pocket of her apron and pulled out a piece of paper, a letter, and handed it to me. "I ran out this morning to grab supplies and found this tucked under your door." I slowly took the letter from her hand before she added, "I, um, didn't want anyone to find it so I—"

"No, no, I get it," I told Lottie. "Thank you." I held the stained parchment in my hand and flipped it over to find it was sealed with wax and admired Lottie for not opening it.

"Who could it be from?" she asked.

I shook my head, eyes unblinking and unable to look away from the envelope. On the back, I found dirty fingerprints and rubbed my thumb over them. Who's could they be? Aside from my crew, I knew no one from that time. No one who'd send me a letter. No one who'd know that I was staying at The Slippery Cod at that very moment.

"I have no earthly idea."

"Well," Lottie prompted and widened her eyes at the paper. "Are you gonna open it? I can go if you need some privacy."

She turned to leave but I grabbed her wrist. I was tired of being alone. "No, stay," I replied and released her arm to slip my finger under the flap and break the wax seal. The paper unfolded to reveal a clumsy scrawl of blank ink and very few words.

*Traveller,*
*The Docks. Twilight. Come alone.*

That was it. Just six little words. Yet, they struck a chord deep in my soul. Tears welled in my eyes as I read them over and over, wondering if Henry had written them. They addressed it to Traveller, careful not to say Time Traveller, Henry's nickname for me. Only he, and those few who found themselves in the forest the night I accidentally broke the snow globe would even know to call me that. It had to be Henry. If anyone were to have survived that horrific night, it had to be him. Then a darker thought flickered across my mind.

What if the letter was from Maria Cobham? What if she was luring me out, alone, to finish what she'd started?

I swallowed hard and folded the letter before tucking it into my jacket pocket. It was a risk I was willing to take. I had a fifty-fifty chance that Henry would be waiting for me at the docks tonight. A sudden glimmer of hope sparked to life in my belly.

"So," Lottie whispered, "who's it from?"

"I'm not sure," I told her. "It wasn't signed. It just asked me to meet them at the docks by twilight."

"Shouldn't be too hard to spot them, then," she

replied. "If it's someone you know. The docks are cleared out by that time. Most of them hangin' around here, drinking themselves silly. Be sure to take a weapon, just in case."

I grew more worried then. If Henry had escaped the Cobhams, he would never ask me to meet him out in the open like that. As much as I wanted it to be him waiting for me... part of me was scared of who I'd find.

# CHAPTER EIGHT

To pass the time, I helped Lottie in the kitchen and set up the tavern to welcome the suppertime rush. She was a surprisingly good cook and I watched her with admiration as she made a massive pot of stew, working the room just like my mother had when I was a girl. All the while, I kept a careful watch on the sun, waiting for it to go down.

Finally, when the sky became stained with a warm glow, I removed the apron Lottie had given me and headed out toward the docks. She was right. Only a few men still hung around, tending to their tiny boats, bustling together in small groups to chit chat about their day on the water. Other than that, the shoreline was quiet and empty aside from the swaying of the anchored ships.

My eyes scanned the area for a familiar figure but found no one. My pulse quickened the further I trailed along, worried for my safety and that of the baby's. I could very well have been walking into a trap, but I realized, after I'd read the letter, a part of me truly knew that Henry was alive. He had to be. I just hoped it was him who'd sent the note.

Just then, I heard the crunching of footsteps in the trees to my left and turned from the docks, heading towards the sounds, my grip tight on the hilt of my sheathed dagger. The footsteps grew closer, but I couldn't see anyone, just the vague outline of something, someone, slowly making their way out of the woods.

My heart wild with fear and anticipation, I called out to them, my mouth quivering. "Who's there?"

Finally, the person emerged and stopped at the treeline, the meager glow of the setting sun barely highlighting the shape of a man. An absurdly tall and broad man, his face cloaked in a black hood. Fear turned to delight, and my heart clawed from the inside, begging to get out and run to him.

"Henry?" I called as I sprinted across the short distance.

His hood flipped back to reveal a face. "Aye, lass," a familiar voice spoke, "it's good to see ye."

I stopped in my tracks to process what I was seeing. My poor heart plunged back into a dark pit. It wasn't Henry. But a new feeling came alive in my chest. Joy. Happiness. My friend was alive.

"Finn?" I cried and ran to him, falling into his open arms and nearly knocking us both down. "You're alive? What are you doing here?"

His massive arms held me tight, but he leaned back to look at my face. His warm grin shone through the thick red beard and his eyes sparkled with amusement. "Aye, I could ask ye the same. I watched ye get sucked into a bloody hole in the air, for Christ's sake."

I laughed but my throat gurgled with a tearful choke. "How did you know I was here? Where I was?"

"I heard whispers of some black-haired devil woman askin' about the likes of our ship," he told me. "Now, I only knows two black-haired devil women," he paused to grin and arch a large red eyebrow at me, "but one of them would surely know the spot she let The Devil's Heart sink."

Our faces both turned solemn, weighed down by the words he spoke. Our home. Our family. They were all gone. I pulled away and stepped back.

"What happened after I was gone?"

Finn's massive frame walked past me and stopped at the edge of the boardwalk, crouching down to take a seat and swing his long legs over the side, dangling over the calm evening water. I followed and sidled up next to him.

"We were all shocked by what happened, when ye," he waved his hand in the air in front of us, "did whatever it is ye did."

I hung my head, staring at my lap. "It was an accident. I was sent—" I stopped myself, but realized there could be no more secrets between us. Finn was my friend, my family. I could trust him with my life. "I was sent back to the future."

The Scotsman's eyes bulged before he let out a sigh and looked out to the calm water. "I knew there was something off about ye." Silence hung in the air, but he soon filled it with a raspy laugh. "It's what saved us, though, ye know?"

I perked up and looked at his face. "What do you mean?"

"Yer little magic show," he replied. "It stunned The Cobhams long enough for us to disarm them. I grabbed little Charlie and high tailed it out of there. I knew Gus and Henry could handle themselves."

I shifted in my spot and grabbed Finn's arm. "Wait, are you telling me Charlie's alive?"

"Aye," he confirmed, but then his face dropped. "Barely."

"What does *that* mean?"

"Maria cut through his neck, but not as deep as it seemed. I carried him out of there and into the village for help. I could hear him breathin'. Hardly. But alive. I got someone to help me clean and sew him up. We've been bunkered down with him, hidin' in the barn of an old friend. But he's," Finn appeared distraught at the thought of Charlie, "Sick."

"Sick?" I shook my head. "What, you mean he's not healing?"

Finn shrugged helplessly. "I don't know. He was doin' fine one day, and then the next he caught a fever, sweatin' all over the place. His wounds turned purple and are festerin'. He hasn't woken up for three days now."

My stomach clenched at the thought. I knew what was wrong. He had an infection. No amount of cleaning and disinfecting would do it at that point. Only one thing could help him. "How far away are you guys?"

"About five hours walkin', give or take." He examined my face curiously. "Why?"

"I have something that can save him," I replied. "And I have a place where you can hide that's better than a barn. He needs to be in a cleaner environment where I can properly tend to his wounds and monitor the fever."

"Aye," he spoke, "I'll see what I can do about gettin' a wagon and a horse."

"And you shouldn't be trekking back to Cupers Over in the dead of night. Stay with me and we can head out tomorrow morning, together." Although I worried about Charlie's life, I was ecstatic at the thought of being reunited with Henry. I beamed. He was *alive*. There was no way I'd wait around The Slippery Cod all day while Finn went to fetch them. "I'm sure Gus and Henry can live without you for one night."

The Scotsman's brow furrowed, and his shoulders hung low. "Oh, Lassie—"

I didn't like his sudden tone. "What?"

"Henry isn't… he's nae with us."

I jumped to my feet and backed away, refusing to believe it. "What are you talking about? You said I distracted The Cobhams so you guys could disarm them."

Finn stood to meet me, arms outstretched to try and calm me. "Now, Dianna—"

"You *said* Gus and Henry could handle themselves." My hands balled into tight fists, the fingernails nearly piercing the flesh of my palms.

"I did," he replied. "I thought they could. But when they didnae turn up, I went back to the spot in the forest. Gus was badly beaten and tied up like a bloody hog. The captain was…"

"What? Was what?" I cried, preparing for the worst.

"Gone," Finn finally said. "They took him. They killed the rest of the crew and set blaze to The Devil's Heart. Now, whether the captain was thrown aboard with it, or if they took him to The Burning Ghost," he shrugged in defeat, "We dinnae ken."

My mouth gaped as I fought back the tears and searched for words. Maria wouldn't do that. Not to her precious pet. No, as much as it killed me to admit it, there was some dark and twisted part of her that cared for Henry. I could see that in her soulless eyes that night. She would have kept him, took him back.

I reached up and vigorously wiped the skin under my tired eyes. "No," I said sternly. "Henry is alive.

And we're going to find him."

***

We snuck back to town and I entered the front of The Slippery Cod while Finn waited out back, hidden in the shadows. The tavern was alive with half-drunk locals and visiting merchants, clanking their mugs of ale and singing jaunty tunes as someone played the fiddle. I made a b-line for the back kitchen, knowing I'd likely find Lottie there. I was right. She tended to the supper dishes over a giant metal tub.

"Hi," she greeted with curiosity, looking me up and down with a half-grin, "How did the secret meeting go?"

I smiled and walked over to her side, lowering my voice to a quiet whisper. "Lottie, I need to know that I can trust you."

She took her hands out of the soapy tub and wiped them on her apron, before tucking a lock of unruly blonde hair behind her ear, her face all serious.

"Well that depends," she replied. "Are you asking if I'm a trustworthy person? Or are you asking me to do something immoral?"

"I would never ask anyone to do something I wouldn't do myself," I assured her, making a mental note of how she didn't seem to like her character being challenged.

She smiled proudly. "Then, yes, you can trust

me." The woman turned and grabbed a couple of fresh buns from the counter and handed one to me before lobbing off a giant bite of her own. "What's the matter? What happened down there? Did you find your captain?"

"Yes and no," I replied vaguely. "It was a friend who'd left the letter. A friend who I thought had died." I took a bite of my bun and spoke with half a mouth. "I need to hide him for tonight. And then tomorrow I'm heading to Cupers Cove to fetch two more of my friends. One of them is a very ill boy. I'll need to hide them here until he recovers. Is that something I can trust you to help me with?"

Lottie didn't respond, only continued to eat her bun and cast curious glances at me from the side. Finally, she spoke. "Are these men dangerous?"

"No, I swear," I quickly blurted out. "They're privateers, one is no more than fifteen years old. He's like a little brother to me. They're good men, I promise you. And they won't be causing any trouble." When she still didn't produce a solid response, I added, "I can pay you for two extra rooms."

She chewed her lip in thought, but then shrugged it off. "Just pay me for one, it's all I have available, anyway. But I can set up a cot in one of the rooms if you need."

My face lit up with joy and I grabbed the woman, bringing her colliding with my body in a clumsy embrace. "Thank you!"

She pushed me away, but the corner of her

mouth turned up. "Did you say you had to hide your friend here tonight?"

"Oh, shoot, yes," I replied, remembering that Finn still waited outside. "He's out back. Is there another exit? I don't want to bring him in through the front and risk him being seen."

She turned and motioned for me to follow. "Can I ask who it is that you're all hiding from?" I watched as she moved some small wooden crates away from a partially hidden door and heaved on the large metal latch that crossed the center.

"Maria and Eric Cobham," I replied. She came to a halt and stared at me with intensity. I couldn't tell if she was angry or surprised, but her eyes narrowed, and her cheeks flushed red. I quickly added, "But I promise, they won't be coming anywhere near the tavern. If we're careful about hiding my friends, they'll never know we're even here."

Lottie didn't reply but her face settled into a stone-cold expression. Did people really fear The Cobhams that much? Or was there something Lottie was hiding from me? She heaved on the door again and it opened with a loud, rusty creak. I peered my head out in search of Finn, but it was pitch black, I couldn't see past where the light escaped from the tavern door. Suddenly, a figure jumped in the doorway from the side and tipped over a small stack of the wooden crates.

"Christ, Lassie," he roared, "I've been freezin' me arse off out there." Finn let out an exaggerated shudder and looked from me to Lottie with an amused grin.

"*This* is your friend?" Lottie asked, eyes wide. "Jesus, good luck keeping him hidden."

I let out a tired sigh. "This is Lottie," I told him. "She's been extremely kind to me and is going to help us stay under the radar while Charlie heals. So, it's a good idea to behave while you're here, understand?" My eyes darted back and forth between the two. "And Lottie, this is Finn."

She nodded. "Clearly not the sick child, then."

He grabbed her hand and bent down to place a kiss on the back of it. "Milady, we are forever in yer debt."

I rolled my eyes but couldn't help laughing. Even in times of crisis, Finn was a shining light. Nothing could keep him down. Lottie didn't seem too pleased by his humor, though. She yanked her hand away, pursed her lips, and turned toward the stairs.

"Follow me."

\*\*\*

Lottie showed Finn to his room and then left abruptly. Something about him made her uneasy, more than her usual everyday unease. Maybe it was his size, or perhaps she had something against Scots. I made a mental note to talk to her later when I had the chance.

"So, tell me more about this time travel bit," Finn

told me as we sat on my bed. I grabbed a few more buns from the kitchen and two bowls of leftover stew. It was cold, but we happily spooned it into our mouths in the quiet echo of my room.

"I don't know how much would make sense to you," I replied honestly. "I mean, I had no idea about any of it until it happened. I still know hardly anything. I've managed to travel back and forth by pure luck, really."

"Nay, I don't believe that." He grabbed another bun and effortlessly bit off an entire half in one bite. "I've never heard of regular people using magic like that. That stuff's only for the fairies and the witches."

"Well, my mom was raised by Martha, the Celtic witch who was in the forest with us that night," I told him. Finn's eyes widened, and I watched as he mindlessly wiped his beard of stew with the palm of his hand. "I had no idea, not until I met her. I didn't even know my mom was from the past."

He nodded. "Aye, the witch. She disappeared the moment ye did."

"Really?"

"Aye, the coward." He gave an exaggerated roll of his eyes "So, where in the past did yer mum come from? And where in the future are ye from, anyway?"

"I was born in 1991, and when you guys scooped me out of the water that day, I'd just come from the year 2018. My mom was—" I realized then, I had no actual idea of where my mom came from. I assumed it was 1707, but she could have come from anywhere in the past. Martha claimed to have raised her, but how long did Celtic witches live? How old was Martha that night I met her? I shrugged. "Actually, I have no idea. She came from the past, that much I know. She washed ashore near my hometown and met my father. Fell in love and stayed there to raise me. But she... drowned when I was younger."

His face softened. "I'm sorry to hear that."

I shrugged. "It was a long time ago. I've dealt with it."

"I knew there was something strange about ye," he added. "That's why I tried to keep ye around. Part of me couldn't bear to see the captain throw ye overboard."

I smiled. "And here we are."

Finn held up his half-eaten bun and I tapped mine to it in a toast. "Aye, here we are." We finished off our food and I set the empty dishes on the tray. "Did Henry know?"

My chest clenched around my heart at the sound of his name. "Yes, he did. Not at first, but I eventually told him. He was going to come to the future with me." My hand rubbed across my stomach, mentally checking on the baby growing inside. My eyes watered over, lips quivering as I fought to keep the tears at bay.

Finn stood and grabbed hold of me, crushing my body to his large frame in a rough and familiar embrace. I took comfort in his friendship. The simple nearness of him was enough to calm me. Finn was like the older brother I never had.

"We'll find him, Dianna. I swear to it."

"I know," I choked out. We lingered in his friendly clasp before I pulled away to wipe the few tears that managed to escape from my eyes. "Where do we start? Do you know where The Cobhams are?"

"Nay," he replied and shook his head. "Everything's been quiet on land and sea since that night. Either they're hidin' out, planning their next attack, or Maria's havin' a time with our captain."

My teeth ground against each other. When we found The Cobham's, I'd kill Maria myself if she hurt a hair on Henry's head. "If things have been quiet, then that probably means they're at sea. Word would travel pretty fast if the crew of The Burning Ghost was staying at a tavern somewhere."

I paced the floor, contemplating our first move after Charlie got better. Then I remembered all the stuff I'd read about Maria during my search for a way back. Books and documents, drawings, so many things Mom had collected on them. I knew all the places Maria liked to hide away, I'd read about the different properties she secretly owned across the province. A smile spread wide across my face. I had everything I needed to find her.

"We set sail. I know a few places we can look."

Finn's chest heaved as he let out a long sigh. "Aye, but it's nae that simple, Lassie. We'd need supplies, food, weapons, and money to buy it all."

He sat down on the bed. "And better yet, we'd need a ship, for Christ's sake."

I was about to open my mouth to speak when the door, which hadn't been fully closed, opened with a creek and Lottie popped her head in. "Sorry," she said, "I was just comin' to fetch your dishes."

"Oh, sure," I grabbed the tray from the dressing table and handed it to her. "Thanks, Lottie."

"I also overheard you sayin' you need a ship," she added with reluctance in her tone.

I raised my eyebrows in surprise. "Uh, yeah, we do. Do you know someone who'd take us aboard theirs? We could pay them."

"No," she replied and folded her arms across her stomach. "But I do know of one you can have."

# CHAPTER NINE

Morning couldn't come fast enough. All night, I'd laid in bed wide awake, thinking about how Lottie could possibly get us a ship. She wouldn't tell us anything the night before, and I didn't want to push. I trusted my friend, and I was thankful for her help. She even offered to loan us her uncle's horse and wagon to go fetch Charlie, to which I was eternally grateful for. Not having to walk through the backwoods of Eastern Newfoundland for five hours was a major sigh of relief.

I loaded up my large satchel and headed next

door to Finn's room before we both slipped downstairs and out the back door. Lottie waited there with the horse and wagon, a heap of blankets in her arms.

"Here," she said, "Use these to hide the giant leprechaun in the back."

"Hey," Finn protested, "I'm a Scot, ye blonde wench."

She rolled her eyes and turned to me. "Just head straight down the main road until you're out of the limits of the village. Stay true to the wider path, you'll make two turns near the end but always choose the wider road. You'll get there."

"Thanks," I told her with sincerity. "If there are no problems, I should be back this evening with the three of them. I'll come here, to the back. So, keep an eye out, okay?" She nodded. "And Charlie will need as many clean linens as you can give me. And hot water. Lots and lots of hot water."

"Got it," she replied and squeezed my shoulder. We exchanged a quick nod and I took the blankets from her grasp. Finn hopped in the back and lay down while Lottie helped me spread the linens over him.

"This is humiliatin'," he muttered.

"Better than getting seen," I told him. "You're just too recognizable."

He let out a feisty harrumph and Lottie chuckled to herself as she headed back inside. "Do ye even know how to drive a wagon? I s'pose ye all ride flying horses where ye come from."

"Geez, I'm from the future, not a different planet," I told him. "But, no, I've never driven a horse-drawn wagon, but I'll figure it out." I nestled a small basket of snacks down next to him and covered his head, attaching the blanket to the back of my seat for security before hopping aboard and grabbing the reins.

We traveled along the wide dirt road towards Cupers Cove, until the constant vibrations of the wooden wheels passing over the gravel became a soothing frequency coursing through my body. Surprisingly, it was in better shape than most Newfoundland roads from my own time, probably from the absence of big trucks and off-road vehicles. The small, brown horse was calm and steady, and I quickly adapted to how the animal reacted to the reins.

Finn talked to me from under the blanket, updating me on more details of what happened after I left. But our conversation quickly turned to placate his curiosity as he began asking a stream of questions about the future. What's it like, what do we eat, where do I live, what do I do? It never ended and I couldn't help but laugh at some of his reactions. He was shocked to learn about ferries and cars and the population of the Earth. I told him Newfoundland eventually becomes part of Canada, breaking away from the rule of the Queen.

The journey felt long, and we only passed a handful of other wagons and people walking. I smiled happily and kept my pace, all the while worried how some people may look at a young woman driving a wagon by herself. To the wrong person, someone with bad intentions, I could look like a tasty target.

My fears were validated when a trio of rough-looking men emerged from the woods in the distance and stopped in the middle of the road. Even from where we were, I could clearly see the shape of swords dangling from their sides.

"Finn," I whispered back over my shoulder, "we have some company. It doesn't look good."

"What are they doing?"

"Standing in a row across the path," I replied.

"Just keep going," he instructed. "Act normal. And whatever ye do, dinnae get down from this wagon."

I held a straight and stern face as our wagon approached the men awaiting us. Up close, I could see just how rough their appearance was. Soiled clothing, torn knees, and blackened skin, no doubt from living outside in the wilderness. These were wild men. And I was in trouble.

I pulled back on the reins and the horse came to a halt. I smiled at them. "Good afternoon, gentlemen." One of them broke away and began circling the wagon. "Can I help you with something?"

"Maybe," the one in the middle replied, his voice torn and raspy. His black hair was oily and curled around his face. I could see the decrepit state of his teeth when he spoke. "What's a pretty little thing like you doing out this far by yourself?"

"On my way to Cupers Cove to see some family," I told them.

The one circling around poked the tip of his sword under the blanket and my heart began to race. These were the type of men who'd no doubt spread the word about Finn's whereabouts, and the news would make its way to Maria in no time.

"Yeah? And what are you bringing along here?"

"Just some old linens and fishing nets for my father," I lied. The wagon jostled as he hoisted himself up on the wheel. I stood in my seat and drew my dagger from its sheath, holding the tip to his neck. "I would appreciate it if you removed yourself from my wagon, sir."

The man stared at me, his dark eyes full of surprise that quickly turned to amusement. He soon held up his hands in mock defeat and stepped down from the wagon. "Apologies, ma'am, I had no idea you were equipped to–" he paused as he sauntered back to join his friends, "defend yourself."

I quirked an eyebrow, dagger still held out in front of me. "Should I need to worry about that?"

The man in the middle, who I realized must have been the leader, stepped forward and wrapped his grubby fingers around the reins I held.

"Why don't you hand these over and step down from your seat?" When I refused to move, he plucked a small blade from inside his jacket and held it to my gut. The hackles on the back my neck stood on end as I thought about the baby, so I slowly obeyed his command. "That's a girl." My feet hit the ground and he held out his free hand, palm up. "And give us the dagger, too, love."

My mind raced to think of a way out before Finn couldn't take it anymore. The last thing we needed was him bursting out of the back like a wild bear and causing a full-on fight. I had too much at stake, I couldn't risk the life of mine and Henry's child against a battle of blades. I glanced down at the dagger in my hand and spotted the insignia of The Burning Ghost, the skull within a flame, and knew these men would no doubt recognize it. I grinned and turned it upright, making sure he wouldn't miss it and handed the dagger over.

"Ah, that's a good girl," he cooed, the words turning my stomach. He let the large knife slip into his palm and I watched his eyes bulge at the sight of the hilt. His face darted back to mine, scared, seemingly fighting to believe what he saw. "Are you—"

"Yes," I told him and stood tall, arms crossed confidently over my torso. He stared me up and down, and I could see the pieces falling into place in his mind as the man began to recognize my likeness to Maria Cobham. "So, I'd suggest you return my dagger and be on your way." I expected him to cower, to scuttle away back into the wood with his friends but was shocked when the street pirate did the opposite. He was pleased as he threw his head back and laughed.

"Jack," he called to one of the other men, "guess what we have here?"

"What?" Jack asked.

"We've got ourselves someone from The Burning Ghost." He came near enough for me to smell the putrid stench of his breath when he cackled quietly, lifting his hand to caress my hair and twist a curl in his fingers. "And I reckon someone close to Maria, by the looks of it." His hand moved to my chin and held it tightly, forcing me to look him in the face. "Do you know what that bitch did to me? To my crew?"

I swallowed hard and attempted to speak through the firm grip he held on my face. "I have some ideas."

"She snuck aboard my ship one night, while we slept. Can you imagine? Too cowardly to take us while we were awake. Jack and I managed to jump overboard and swim away." He paused to take a deep breath. "Not far enough, though. We still had to watch our ship, our crew, go up in flames and sink to the God damn ocean floor." He gave another squeeze before letting my face go. "She took everything away from me. But now," he laughed, "we have *you*."

My lungs struggled to keep a steady breath and my veins ran hot with fear. The leader looked over my shoulder and gave a curt nod to the one named Jack. Before I could turn around, the man had grabbed me from behind, holding my arms too tight as they pulled at the sockets of my shoulders.

I tried to stifle the scream that I held in my throat as the not yet healed stitches stretched and the new flesh burned.

"What should we do with her, Amos?" Jack asked the leader as he pressed his body against my back. I could feel him getting aroused from the excitement and it made me want to vomit.

Amos flipped my dagger around and pressed the tip to my belly. His face twisted into an evil grin when it elicited a slight yelp from me. Did I dare tell them I was with child? Would they care? Would it make his act of revenge even worse?

"Can't just kill you," he noted. "We gotta send a message. Maybe I'll gut you here on the road and leave a trail of your blood back to Kelly's Island."

Enough was enough, I couldn't defend myself against all three men. "Finn!" I screamed, startling the street pirates.

I took the split-second opportunity to raise my leg and plant a heavy foot in Amos's stomach, pushing me back and away from the knife. Finn came barrelling out of the wagon like a crazed animal, sword drawn, and growling as he jumped to the ground with a loud thud. Jack continued to back away, still holding his grip on my arms.

I threw my head back as hard as I could, knocking into his face. I could feel his teeth cut through my scalp and my mind spun from the impact. But it worked. He let me go. I ran toward Amos, grabbed my dagger that he'd dropped on the ground and, without a second thought, sliced through the back of his leg.

The man screamed in pain and grabbed at his appendage as he crumbled to the ground. Finn held off the other two with sheer intimidation. They held their hands up in defeat and pleaded for their lives.

"Just kill me, then," Amos told me, desperation in his tone.

"I'm not a murderer," I replied which caused a guffaw from the man. "Seriously. I have Maria's dagger, but I'm not part of her crew. I swear to it."

"Why should I believe you?" he asked and winced in pain.

I sheathed my knife. "You don't have to. But I hope that our mercy is enough to prove it. Maria would never let a soul go free and you know it." I bent down to his eye level. "Look, I'm sorry for what she did to you. But she did the same to me. Trust that I despise her just as much as you do." I glanced at his leg, the blood had already soaked through his dirty pants. "Keep this as clean as possible. Wrap it tight. You'll be fine." I stood and began walking back to the wagon, signaling Finn to come. He grunted and followed, sword still pointed at the other two men.

"I owe you a debt, then," Amos called after me. I stopped and looked back over my shoulder in confusion. "You spared my life, I must repay the debt."

I looked at Finn, pursing my lips as I thought about it. He leaned and whispered, "Ye could tell him to keep his filthy mouth shut."

I smiled and turned my attention to Amos. "All I ask is that you never speak a word of this. To anyone. *Ever*." I let out a heavy sigh. "Is that something you can do?"

Amos chuckled. "What? Keep it a secret that me and my men were taken down by a *woman*?" He waved me off. "Go on, get on your Jesus wagon and get outta here."

Finn and I hopped aboard, and I whipped the reins, signaling the horse to get going. We left the street pirates in a cloud of sandy dust and I sighed in relief as we got further and further away.

"Aye, remind me not to mess with ye," Finn said jokingly and slid over the back of my seat to take his hiding place under the blanket. "We should hurry, though. Men like that aren't likely to keep their word."

"You don't think so?"

"I know they ain't."

I flicked the reins once again, harder, and our trusty horse picked up its pace. The ride became rough and bumpier, but we had to hurry. Time was not our friend.

I'm not sure it ever was.

# CHAPTER TEN

We neared the community of Cupers Cove ahead of schedule and Finn told me to bypass the main road that entered it. The farm property where they'd been hiding was just outside of the town, but not far. I hauled back on just one of the reigns and our trusty horse obeyed, taking the turn with ease. Soon, the line of an old farmhouse appeared in the distance. Next to it, a barn, surprisingly large and covered in wood siding that had been greyed and weather from the ocean.

Finn pulled back the low canopy and hauled himself over the back of my seat. "Stop here."

I gently reigned in the horse and we came to a halt just outside the barn's large front doors. Finn hopped down and then motioned for me to follow. We entered the dimly lit structure and I followed Finn over to the far corner where I could hear the faint hum of a voice. As we got closer, I could make out the low and bristly tone of Gus.

"Gus!" I called and ran to wrap my arms around him from behind. The man, startled, whipped around in my grip and pushed me away. But when his eyes widened at the sight of me, he quickly brought me back in and hugged me tightly.

"Christ," he muttered, "where have you *been*?" We broke free from one another and he looked to Finn. "So, you were right, then?"

"Aye," Finn replied. "I knew it had to be her. I was careful, though. Nobody saw me."

Gus nodded and then turned his attention back to me. He never smiled, but his eyes sparkled with eager curiosity. "It's good to see ya." He heaved a big sigh and I knew what he wanted to ask. Where did I go? What happened that night? But he refrained.

I smiled and nodded. "It's good to see you, too."

But my happiness quickly faded when I spotted a body laying on a heap of hay covered in linens. Charlie. I pushed past Finn and Gus to kneel at his side and took his bony hand in mine. It was boiling hot. They had him stripped down to his bare chest, only his legs covered by a thin sheet. His pale and sickly skin was drenched in sweat. My eyes went straight to his neck where I knew Maria's sword had sliced through it, noting the yellowed cloth that had been wrapped around it and how it was soaked in a rainbow of colors; yellow, red, purple, and green. I reached over and gently lifted the side of the bandage and gagged at the putrid smell that immediately wafted across my nose.

"He's seriously infected," I told the other two. "I'll need to clean this before we hit the road. We can't risk traveling with him in this state. I need clean cloths and hot water. As hot as you can get it. And some kind of soap, if it's possible."

Gus looked at Finn and nodded his head toward the door. "Go fetch the lady of the house and see what she can get for ya."

"Aye." Finn nodded and ran off.

I leaned in and cupped little Charlie's clammy cheek in my hand. He was more boy than man and it pained me to see him like that, just laying there, unaware of the world around him and the state he was in. I listened to his labored breaths and how they slightly choked as they passed through his throat. It was a wonder he was still alive.

"So," Gus spoke, breaking the silence of the echoing barn. "What happened back there that night?" I looked over my shoulder, watching as he came and squatted down next to me.

"It's a long story," I replied. "But, I went back to where I came from."

His face twisted in confusion, his big brown eyes pleading. "Why would you just leave us like that?"

I'd never witnessed Gus portray emotion other than anger and sheer discontent for my existence. We tolerated one another, at best. But there in the barn, I could see the layer underneath. The layer that actually did care for me, considered me family the way I did for him.

"I'm sorry," I honestly told him. "I never meant to do it. It happened by accident."

He rubbed his beard and nodded, but he still didn't seem convinced.

"I tried everything in my power to get back here, though. Please, know that. I sacrificed everything for the slightest chance to come back. If I could change what happened, I would in a heartbeat."

"No," he blurted. "It's what saved us."

"Right, yeah, Finn told me." The tears began to well and I fought them back. "But did it really?"

"What do you mean?"

"Look at poor Charlie. And… *Henry*." My voice cracked, and I choked on my words.

Gus patted his hand on my back. "Don't think like that. Henry's alive. I know it." He let a pause hang in the air. "And so do you, don't ya?"

I gave him a weak and quivering smile. "Yeah, I do."

But, if Maria had him, being alive may not be a good thing. I imagined him aboard her ship, wishing for death to come and release him from the torture. A shiver washed over my body and I stood to get away from it.

"Aye, Lassie," Finn called from the door. He marched through the barn with a large metal pan full of steaming hot water, clean linens draped over his shoulder. He set it down next to Charlie and handed me the white cloths. "Will this do?"

"Yes, it's perfect," I told him. I grabbed an empty milk pail and turned it upside down, placing it next to Charlie and took a seat. First, I rolled up my sleeves as high as they could go and then washed my own skin, paying close attention to the underside of my nails.

Next, I took a deep breath before leaning in to remove his soiled bandages. All three of us gagged from the smell. It reminded me of when I finally got my cast removed from my arm when I'd broken my wrist in junior high. I'd never forgotten the raunchy stench of dead skin and sweat. This was so much worse. I imagined it to be as close to the smell of a dead body as you could get without actually being dead. Some scabbing and crusted yellow puss came away with the bandage, causing fresh blood to fill the wound.

"Good God," Finn muttered. "The poor bugger."

"You guys can leave if you want," I told them.

"Nay," Finn replied. "I've smelled worse."

I worked fast and steady, careful not to open the wound too much, but determined to remove as much of the infection as I could. It was hard, the stitching job that had been done in haste to save Charlie was jagged and sloppy. I wasn't sure if it helped or did more harm, but it did keep his skin together.

When I'd finished, I wiped some of my rubbing alcohol around the wound and then tore the linens into small strips to wrap around his neck. Through it all, Charlie never budged, never woke up. Lastly, I crushed up one of my antibiotic pills on an upturned wooden crate and brushed the dust into a warm glass of water that had been sitting there. I tipped the boy's head back and opened his mouth to gently pour the water down. When I was sure it had all slid down his throat, I stood and turned to find an awestruck Finn and Gus.

"We should hit the road," I informed them. They never asked questions, never spoke a word of the foreign things I'd pulled from my satchel. Something deep inside of me warmed at the thought of how much they must have trusted me.

Gus found four scraps of wood, nailed them to the inside corners of the wagon and then fashioned a canopy from some of the blankets. "There, now we can sit in the back with the boy and stay hidden on the road."

The two of them jumped in the back and I hopped in the driver's seat again, grabbing the reins and giving them a sharp flick. We were off, heading back over the road we came in on, only much faster this time. The high afternoon sun made us vulnerable and I worried the entire way back about the street pirates we encountered. Would they still be there? Would there be others?

Had they kept their word or did they run off in search of The Cobhams to tell them all about the black-haired woman and Scot who took them down?

My fears subsided as the rocky landscape became more and more familiar. Tall, Evergreen trees thickened the forests on each side. I knew we were approaching the town limits of Harbour Grace and I longed to be under the cover of my bedroom at The Slippery Cod. I took the back road that Lottie had showed me and brought the wagon to the back door. She must have been watching for us because my friend came running out before the horse even came to a full halt.

"You made it," she said by way of greeting. "I take it there were no problems, then?"

"Oh, no," I replied and jumped down from my seat. "We definitely had problems. Some street pirates stopped us about halfway."

"Oh?" Lottie turned her attention to the canopy and quirked her eyebrow.

"We got away," I told her. "And sorry, we needed something better to hide them. I can have Gus take it down, don't worry."

The two men then emerged from the back of the wagon, each holding an end of Charlie who was still unconscious but appeared to be less sweaty already. I breathed a sigh of relief.

"Aye," Finn grunted to Lottie, "can ye opened the door?"

She rolled her eyes but then they widened at the

sight of the young boy. She paused for a brief moment and then scurried to open the big wooden door for the two men.

"Bring him up to your room, Finn," she instructed.

We all filed in and up the stairs to the bedrooms. Lottie had set up a cot in Finn's room and stacked a pile of clean linens next to the wash pan.

"Thank you," I told her.

She smiled and nodded. "I set up the cot here, I have one more if you'd like it for your room. Two just won't fit in here."

"That would be great, thanks," I replied and glanced at Finn. "Guess we're bunkmates again."

"At least this time I don't have to put up with ye bloody tossin' and turnin'," he replied jokingly.

They'd gently laid Charlie down on the bed and situated him. He didn't wake but let out a slight moan. The two men brightened.

"That's the most sound he's made in days," Gus told us. "Looks like your magic is workin'."

I felt my cheeks flush red. "It's not magic, it's—" I was very aware of Lottie's curious eyes on me. "It's medicine. Where I come from, it's used to make sick people better. Charlie should be fine in a few days if he's not too far gone. We just won't know until then." A tired sigh escaped my body and I turned to Lottie. "That gives us time to get the ship ready. Are we still good there? Can we at least see it?"

"Aye, we're gonna need more than a wee

schooner, Lassie," Finn piped in.

Lottie rolled her eyes in annoyance and stomped over to the window overlooking the docks outside. "There," she said and pointed, "that one. It's all yours, on one condition."

We all leaned in and peered out the window, trying to see which ship she spoke of. The harbour was half-filled with boats of all sizes, but they were mostly small fishing vessels, none big enough for the journey ahead of us. For life at sea.

All except for one, that is.

A large, three-mast structure sat in the water far in the distance, away from all the other ships. Painted red with gold trims and a massive stern hanging off the back. It was like a giant ruby in a sea of pebbles out there, all alone, too big to come any further into the harbor. No wonder there were men wanting to buy it. I couldn't imagine the pretty penny it would fetch to the right buyer.

Gus's eyes bulged. "That's a bloody full-rigged ship."

"Where the Christ did you get a ship like that?" Finn asked her.

"It was my grandfather's," she answered. "He gave it to my father before heading back to England and I used to go sailing with him all the time." She crossed her arms tight and looked down at the floor. "I miss it. Since their deaths, I haven't been able to bring myself to step foot aboard it. Not that I could sail it myself, anyway. No one will sail it with me. Every God damn man in town wants it, but they won't use it for what it's meant for."

"And what's that?" I asked, stunned by the new information.

She looked at me and smirked with her eyebrows raised, something alive shining through that I never witnessed her express before. "Adventure."

"Wait, hang on," Gus cut in and then cast another glance at the massive ship, his eyes growing wide. "I recognize... *who* was your grandfather?"

She pursed her lips and stared at us for a moment before saying, "John Roberts."

Finn began sputtering off Scottish curse words and plunked down on the bed. Gus tried hard to hide his shock but failed. I, however, had no idea what was going on.

Gus pointed out the window. "That right *there* is the God damn Queen."

I shook my head in confusion. "What?"

"The Queen, captained by the infamous Red John Roberts, part of Peter Easton's fleet of ships." He sauntered over to Lottie and looked her straight in the eye. "Which makes your father Red Jack Roberts and *you*," he stopped to chortle, "You're bloody Charlotte Roberts, aren't ya?"

"Yes, so what?" she challenged.

I deeply admired her bravery, even though Gus was no one to fear. He was just a grump. But Peter Easton...he was pirate royalty. He ruled most of Newfoundland, became one of the most elusive and successful pirates of his time. Perhaps of all time.

"Do you want the ship or not?"

Gus's face broke into a fit of laughter, a strange image for me to see coming from him. "You expect us to believe you're just gonna *give* us one of the most coveted pirate ships on the bloody island?"

"Yes," she replied. "No one will sail it with me because I'm a woman. It deserves to be at sea."

Finn stood then. "Lassie, we appreciate the gesture, but everythin' comes at a price. And it's a price we cannae afford."

"I didn't say you could have it for free," she told us. "But I don't want money."

"Well, what do you want?" I asked.

I watched as she chewed her bottom lip in thought. "Take me with you."

The men erupted into more laughter.

"Look," Gus cut to a serious face, "we can't go takin' all sorts of women out on the sea. It's a bad fortune. Dianna's lucky, she has somethin' to offer. As pretty as you are—"

"Well, it's a good thing it's not your decision to make, now, is it?" Lottie blurted out. Gus appeared confused as she continued, "I'm not giving the ship to *you*." She turned to face me and smiled triumphantly. "I'm giving it to Dianna."

Eyes wide and brows high, I spoke with a laugh, "Uh, what?"

Lottie folded her arms tightly and held her head high. "That's right. The Queen is all yours, Captain."

# CHAPTER ELEVEN

Lottie, Finn, and I sat in a small boat as we rowed out to The Queen. A temperamental Gus stayed behind to watch over Charlie, but really, I knew he was mad about the whole boat and me being captain thing. As much as I adored the man, he was so stubborn and old-fashioned, even for this era. I didn't know much about his past, other than the fact that Maria had taken everything from him when she burned his ship and murdered his crew. But I wondered then, of Gus's life before that. Had he been married? Kids? Daresay... happy?

I set my thoughts aside as we came up broadside of the ship, a massive red sea beast with yellow trims. I stared in wonder at the portholes lining the sides and the mouths of cannons poking out in between. I counted six that I could see, assuming there were six more to match on the other side of her. A thick rope ladder hung down from the edge and dangled near the bottom where our little rowboat pulled up. Finn grabbed hold of it and pulled us close, so we could climb on.

I struggled at first, maintaining my footing in the rocky boat while I secured my grip around the itchy rope, but I climbed the length of it with ease until I reached the top and Finn helped haul me over the edge.

My leather boots hit the upper deck with a loud thud and I stared around me in utter awe. Heaps of spooled rope, giant metal anchors, and wooden crates covered in heavy nets were placed throughout. An impressively sized steering wheel sat near two staircases that led to the deck above the stern.

I walked over to it and placed my hands on the girthy handles, admiring the craftsmanship and noting a gorgeous compass built into the pedestal. I looked up and glanced around. This was a ship to be feared. This was a ship to be revered.

And it was mine.

"Aye, lass," Finn called as he climbed up from the deck below. "'Tis a beauty, she is. We'll do some fine sailin' aboard her." He stopped when he saw where I stood and grinned from ear to ear, stepping back to size me up. Then he heaved a happy sigh. "Ye look good there, ye know."

I smiled. "Thanks. I just hope Gus can get on board with the idea of me being his captain." I stepped away and walked over to him. "I mean, I'll need the both of you if I'm to do this right. I have no clue what I'm doing."

"Yes ye do," my friend replied. "Ye were born fer it. The sea loves ye. Gus will be fine, just let him suck his own teat for the day."

I laughed and slapped him on the arm. "Where's Lottie?"

He thumbed over his shoulder. "Checking out the kitchen, seein' what we need. I took some stock, meself. We're gonna need some weapons, supplies and the lot." He eyeballed the cannons that lined each side. "I reckon we won't be needin' cannonballs, The Burning Ghost ain't got cannons. But it might be smart to have some onboard." He threw me a wink. "Just in case."

I nodded, filing the information away in my mind. Being the captain of a ship wasn't too different from owning your own business, I imagined. You're responsible for your employees, inventory, supplies, not to mention profits. We had to find a way to make money, and I didn't fancy the idea of piracy. Not of innocent people, anyway.

Just then, Lottie emerged from the same ladder Finn climbed up from and walked over to where we stood. She held a long parchment in her hand. "I've made a list of all the supplies we'll need for the kitchen. Should do us a while at sea."

Finn cleared his throat uncomfortably. "Uh, Lassie, readying a ship this size for the sea is goin' to cost a pretty penny."

"No worries," I dug around in my satchel for the bag of schillings I'd brought and pulled it out, holding it up for them to see. "I came prepared."

Finn's eyes bulged. "Where the Christ did ye get all that money?"

"My, um, my mother saved this for a lot of years. It was just collecting dust back home. Better to be here, where it can actually be used, right?"

The Scot's eyes quickly darted to Lottie and then back again. "Right. Yes. Good of yer mother to be so savvy."

Lottie leaned in. "Am I missing something here?"

"No," I assured her. "Just... my mother died when I was younger. It's sometimes hard to talk about her." I was flat out lying to my friend, but too many people already knew my secret and I wasn't totally sure I could trust Lottie yet. Not with something like that. If the wrong person knew I had the ability to travel through time... who knew what could happen. "So, where do we go to get what we need?"

"Well, I can get everything to stock the pantry. I have some chickens and a goat we can take from the tavern. I just have to clean the tiny stable aboard the ship. And I can just wash the linens already aboard instead of spending money on new ones," Lottie offered.

"Gus would be the man to collect the other

things we need," Finn added. "I'd like to spend a day aboard, makin' sure everything runs smoothly, check the sails and the lot."

"Okay, let's head back, talk to Gus, and get as much done today as we can." I looked up at the sky, squinting from the high afternoon sun. "We still have some daylight left. I'd like to sail as soon as possible."

"Aye," Finn paused, his beard scrunching up into a grin, "*captain*."

I laughed and shoved at his shoulder. "Shut up."

"Wait," Lottie spoke, "you haven't seen the best part." She began walking over toward the door to the stern. The captain's quarters.

My heartbeat kicked up a notch at the idea of it being *my* quarters. I watched as she turned the large brass knob, then heaved on the hefty wooden door and followed her in. It was dimly lit, the curtains were drawn shut, but through the filtered light of the sun shining through, I could see a stunning bedroom and office area.

A double bed sat nestled in a built-in nook, much like Henry's aboard The Devil's Heart, only this one was adorned with gorgeous hand-carved embellishments. A red velvet sofa with a tufted back sat on the opposite side, near the door. A short, but long, bookcase filled with books next to it. In the center sat a large mahogany desk, with bold claw foot legs and gold hardware. I walked over and pulled out the wingback chair, upholstered in the same red velvet as the sofa, and sat down.

"Looks good on ye," Finn said, his words echoing off the quiet walls.

I should have been ecstatic, I should have been in my glory. But a heavy pit in my stomach wouldn't let go of the infinite sadness that turned around in there. Like a ball in perpetual motion, the pain of Henry's absence fueled my sorrow.

I peered up at him. "It feels wrong without him."

He breathed a sigh and looped his thumbs through the hoops on his belt. "Aye, I know, lass. But we'll find him. We'll get Henry back and then ye two can rule this ship together."

Lottie came around the desk and placed her hand on my shoulder. "We all will," she told me. "I know the shores of this island like the back of my hand. I practically lived on this ship growing up. We sailed everywhere. We'll search every nook and cave."

I nodded and smiled, hiding the warm tears that sat behind my eyes, ready to pour out. How did I get so lucky to fall into a friendship with someone like Finn and Gus? Any pirate ship could have plucked me from the sea that day. And then Lottie. Time saw fit to insert me into situations where I walked right into the perfect people. Lottie, I hardly knew her, but our friendship felt real. I knew it would only grow into something beautiful over the years. Like kindred spirits. I wondered then if my time traveling adventures had anything to do with my ties back to piracy. Maria Cobham was my blood relative. Did blood call to blood? Was she the reason the siren let me bend the laws of time? Or was I destined to come back and cross fateful paths with Lottie? The granddaughter of Red John Roberts, one of Peter Easton's...

My eyes widened and shot back and forth between my two friends.

"Are you okay?" Lottie asked.

The sudden idea washed over my body and fit into place like missing pieces of a puzzle. It felt so right. "I know where The Cobhams are."

Finn stepped forward. "What? Are ye sure?"

"Yes," I told him. "remember the street pirates?"

"Aye."

"When Amos had the knife held to my stomach, he said that he wanted to send a message to Maria. That he should just gut me right then and leave a trail of blood back to Kelly's Island."

I could see the cogs slowly clicking into place, but he needed more. I looked at Lottie. "And what's Kelly's Island known for?"

She thought for a second and then her face lit up. "That's where Peter Easton stationed his headquarters. It's been abandoned for years. But it's the perfect place to hide from the world while keeping eyes on the shores all around. You couldn't sneak up from anywhere."

"No," I replied. "But we will. We'll form a plan and go to Kelly's Island." I slammed my hand down on the desk. *My* desk. "We're going to save Henry."

\*\*\*

After we rowed back to shore, I scrambled out of the small boat and the three of us practically ran back to The Slippery Cod. We found Gus watching over young Charlie who was looking so much better. His pale skin was free of sweat but still felt hot to the touch.

"He stirred for a while," Gus told us proudly. "Never woke, but at least he's in there somewhere."

I crushed up another antibiotic pill and dissolved it in water before carefully pouring it down Charlie's throat. I slipped the bottle back in my satchel and looked to my friends.

"He needs two per day just like I did there. He should wake up once the fever goes down enough." I reached over and touched the back of my hand to his forehead again. "Which it already is. Hopefully, he'll be in good enough shape when we're ready to sail."

"Speakin' of which," Finn piped in and stepped toward Gus, "we all got jobs to do."

Gus nodded. "I figured. What do you require of me?"

I pulled out the bag of schillings and handed it to him. I could have given it to Lottie back on the ship, but I wanted a way to win over Gus's approval. Trusting him with a large amount of money and managing the readying of our ship should do the job. "Go with Lottie. Get everything we need. I'll stay with Charlie and Finn has some things to do aboard The Queen."

He slowly accepted the heavy pouch of money, a thoughtful look on his face.

"I'm going to really need you, Gus," I told him. "I can't do this without you. I need the best quartermaster on the sea, and you're it."

He sighed, but I could see the smallest hint of a smile behind his scruffy brown beard. "Fine," he said. "But we'll need a crew. Deckhands. We can't manage that beast just the four of us."

"I trust you to find some capable bodies," I told him, further offering my trust in him. It was working. I could see the sense of pride and purpose coming to the surface of his demeanor.

"Right," he replied and looked at Lottie. "And you know where to go for everything?"

She grinned. "I can point you in the right direction, sure." She turned on her heel and strut out the door, calling behind her, "Come on then! I'm not gonna hold your hand."

I chuckled but my laughter turned to surprise when I spotted the slight hint of a red color flush to Gus's cheeks. Our eyes met, and the redness spread. But he stormed out before I could say anything.

"Well, this should be an interesting adventure," I muttered to myself as I walked over and sat down in the armchair next to Charlie.

I watched him for hours, dripping small spoonfuls of soup broth down his throat in an attempt to feed some nutrients into him. His frail body shifted ever so slightly and his face twisted into all sorts ways. He was in there, that was for sure. We just had to give the medicine time to work. In just one day, I could already see a huge improvement, and that was a great sign.

I held his hand and talked to him as if he were awake. Telling him all about my journey back to the future, and retelling my adventures with The Devil's Heart through my eyes. How scared I was at first, and how he was one of the first to show me kindness.

"I never did thank you for trying to save me from Maria," I finally told him. "I'll never forgive myself for what she did to you. I'm so sorry, Charlie." I glanced down at my belly and lovingly rubbed my hand over it. "I have a secret," I told him in a low whisper. "I'm carrying Henry's baby. I know, crazy, right? I haven't told anyone, but I know I can trust you." I kept his small hand in mine and leaned forward to rest my head on the bed.

Before long, I had drifted off, and awoke to a dark room, Charlie sleeping soundly. I noticed that his breathing had become less labored and took a sigh of relief as I listened to the soft, relaxed inhale and exhale of air from his body. I reached up and felt his forehead, too. It was warm, but not burning hot like earlier. The antibiotics were working hard and fast.

I roamed The Slippery Cod in search of my tiny crew and found Lottie in the kitchen, cleaning up from the supper rush. I noted a huge pile of linens on the floor in the corner and more dishes piled on the counters than usual. She was bent over the washtub, scrubbing pots so I walked over.

"Here, let me do that," I told her.

She shook the suds from her hands and stepped back. "Thanks, my hands were starting to turn to prunes."

"Is this all stuff from the ship?"

"Most of it," she replied. "I'm still cleaning up from the supper rush."

"Lottie, who's going to watch over the tavern when you come with us?"

"I've already talked to my cousin. She and her husband are more than happy to run it in my absence," she told me as she began sorting through the pile of linens.

"And your uncle won't care?"

I caught her rolling her eyes. "My uncle has been in England for four years. No one expects him to come back anytime soon. The tavern has been in the family for years, and he's got his own business to tend to over there. He runs a farm that supplies most of the food for the Queen of England."

I didn't even bother to hide my look of surprise. "Wow, yeah, why would someone ever leave that?"

"Exactly," she agreed. "The Slippery Cod is a town staple, everyone relies on it, travellers love it. As long as someone is here to cook the food, serve the rum, and make the beds, no one will bat an eye."

I focused my attention on the dishes as my friend

worked the linens on a scrub board. We spent the better part of an hour like that, silently performing duties, enjoying one another's easy company.

Finally, after a while, I had to ask, "Lottie, I really am thankful for the ship."

"It's no problem," she replied. "It needs a captain. It should be out there on the sea."

"I can't help but wonder, though," I said as I added the last of the dishes to the soapy water, "why you wouldn't captain it yourself."

Lottie stopped and stared at me, confusion with a hint of offense on her face. "I told you, no one would sail with me."

"But we would. I don't have to captain it. The boys and I would be just as happy catching a ride."

I watched as she returned her attention to the scrub board, crushing the fabric against it with a bit too much force. "I don't want to captain The Queen."

"But, really, it's yours—"

"I said I don't want to captain it, Dianna!" Frustration exploded from her in a quick burst, but she soon cooled and tucked a few stray blonde curls behind her ears. "It's too much responsibility. I thought... I thought I could trust you to do it."

I held my hands up in defeat. "You can. I will."

Lottie sighed and seemed to relax, but then appeared to retreat deeper in thought.

"Is there something else on your mind?" I dared asked her as I dipped the final dirty pan into the water. "Did Gus give you any trouble today?"

Her cheeks flushed, much like Gus's had earlier, and she hid her face from me. "No, no, Gus was a perfect gentleman," she assured me and began wringing out a wet sheet through an ancient contraption with a turn crank.

I played devil's advocate. "You know, I think he likes you."

"Oh?" she replied and mindlessly continued her task.

She scooped up a pile of wrung out sheets and headed out the back door, I assumed to hang them on the line to dry in the cool night air. I laughed and followed her out there to help.

For a woman with a hard exterior, a part of Lottie was soft and accepting of our friendship. For that, I would be forever grateful.

*** 

The next day, Finn and Gus were gone when I awoke, probably eager to have a purpose and a goal of getting our ship sea ready. I found Lottie outside, tending to the never-ending clothesline. I tipped my head up to the warm morning sun and inhaled deeply the scent of fresh linens blowing in the breeze. It was odd, that three hundred years in the past, the scent was so familiar to me. There was nothing better than crawling into bed after Mom had dried the sheets on the line.

"Morning, sleepyhead," Lottie called over to me.

I squinted from the bright sun and smiled at her

from under the cover of my hand across my brow. I walked over to my friend and helped her straighten out a wet blanket she'd thrown over the line. "Sleepyhead?"

Lottie began pinching wooden clothespins on the quilted blanket and peered at me from the other side. "Yeah, it's nearly time to get ready for the lunch rush."

My eyes widened. "How did I sleep for so long?"

She kept peering at me, glancing from the corners of her vision as she continued her laundry task. "I'm not sure," she replied jokingly, "you've been sleeping like a pregnant woman if you ask me." When I didn't answer she stopped fussing with the pins and threw her hands to her hips. "Why didn't you tell me?"

I shrugged. "I dunno. You didn't want any trouble, and I wasn't sure if I could trust you yet."

She appeared offended at the last part, but quickly brushed it off. "A baby is no trouble, Dianna. It's a blessing."

"I know, I know," I told her. "I just—"

"And I know we've only known each other for a few days, but you can trust me. I wouldn't hand over my life and my ship to you if you couldn't. If I didn't trust *you*."

I hadn't thought of it that way and I hung my head. Silence filled the space between us, the only sound that of the sheets flapping in the wind and the seagulls down by the docks. I picked up a sheet and threw it over the line.

"I'm sorry."

"It's fine," she replied. "But you need to start trusting me if this is going to work."

"I know. I will. I do," I rambled and then sucked in a deep breath. "I really do."

Lottie didn't falter from her task, but she cast a grinning look over the line. "When are you due?"

"I'm pretty early," I told her, surprisingly happy to talk about my little miracle with someone. "But we should expect the little one in about eight months."

"Are you scared?"

I swallowed hard. "Yes."

"If it helps ease your mind, I've aided in the delivery of four healthy children," she told me. "for women in town."

I brightened. "Actually, that does put some of my worries to rest." I pinched the last clothespin on the line. "I'm going to go check on Charlie," I added. "Did you need me to help out with the lunch crowd?"

"No, it's fine. My cousin is coming to help."

"Okay," I replied, "I'll talk to you later, then."

I walked back inside with a sense of guilt. Lottie was a hard person to crack, but she obviously considered us friends and I'd hurt her feelings. An idea came to life in my mind and I headed upstairs to her room. I pulled my diamond studs from my satchel, the ones I caught her admiring when I'd first arrived, and placed them in a tiny dish on her dresser with a note that said, *for my friend*.

I then made my way over to the room where

Charlie was and gently opened the door, peeking my head inside. I saw the slightest hint of movement on the pillow of the bed and fully entered the room to find the boy conscious.

"Charlie! You're awake!"

I took a wide stride to his side and sat down.

He looked tired, pale, and in desperate need of a bath. But still, he appeared to be miles better than he did just barely two days ago. His mouth gaped but no words came out, only a strained and muffled sound.

"Shh," I told him and scooped his hand into mine. "Don't. You're still healing. It's best if you refrain from speaking for a while."

He nodded and then seemed to relax back into his pillow, a smile spread wide on his face, eyes sparkling as they locked onto mine.

"What?" I asked. "Are you happy to see me?"

He nodded again.

"I'm so sorry. I'm sorry for what Maria did to you, for leaving when I did, for... everything." Thin tears rained down my face, but I let them.

I could tell Charlie wanted to speak so badly, his hands moved in the air as if they could talk for him, working with his eyes to convey what he thought. I reached into my satchel and pulled out a notepad and pencil, then offered it to the boy.

He quickly scribbled some words at the top and turned the pad back to me to reveal the words, *where did you go*?

"I went back to where I came from," I told him as

honestly as I could. "But I didn't mean to. I didn't want to leave you guys."

He scratched something else down. *Henry?*

The tears warmed and flowed heavily then, but I kept a smile on my face. "He's... gone. The Cobhams took him."

He underlined the word *where* and widened his eyes, almost in anger.

I shrugged. "We don't know for certain, but there's a good chance he's on Kelly's Island. We're sailing there tomorrow."

More scribbling. *What can I do to help?*

I laughed when I read it and remembered something Henry once told me, that Charlie was unstoppable, eager to help, and loved the sea.

"Don't worry, we're not going anywhere without you," I assured him. "But you need to rest until we leave. Even then, you'll be resting on the ship, too."

He didn't seem too happy with that but must have been too tired to argue otherwise because he set the items down on the bed and closed his eyes, inhaling deeply.

"I'm going to go get you some soup, okay?" I stood to leave, my sense of hope greater than it was earlier.

I'd traveled back through time, found my friends, acquired my own ship, and saved Charlie's life. I felt unstoppable. There was only one thing left to do and nothing would stand my way. Something warmed in my belly at the thought. This time tomorrow, I'd be well on my way to saving the man

I loved.

# CHAPTER TWELVE

I stood at the bowsprit of The Queen, my ship. *My* ship. At first, I had found myself wandering its decks repeating the words to myself. My kitchen, my quarters, my ship. But we'd been at sea for a few hours and everyone was settling into the new roles aboard the vessel.

Gus had managed to scoop up three young deckhands, not much older than Charlie. But if there were anything like him, we would be just fine. The cool sea breeze misted across my face and the warm sun beamed down. I tilted my head and closed my eyes, dreaming of a time not so long ago when I did the same aboard The Devil's Heart.

"Ye missed it," Finn spoke from behind me.

I turned to him. "Yeah, I did. I do." I inhaled deeply. "I love the sea."

"Aye, not everyone's built fer it." He stepped closer and placed his hands on the railing. "I'd live and die on the sea, nothin' would make me happier. She's my lady."

I grinned. "I thought you didn't fancy the curvy body of a woman?" I mocked him, repeating some of the first words he ever spoke to me.

Finn coughed out a raspy laugh and adjusted his big leather belt. "Aye, that's cause there's only one woman for me. Her rollin' waves are all the curves I need."

I laughed but then turned to business. "So, when do we make landfall to our destination?"

The Scot's eyes widened with his raised brows and he leaned back from me. "Well, well," he quipped, "Aren't we the little captain?"

I rolled my eyes. "Please don't make this any harder than it is. I'm trying to be an authority."

"Whatever that means." Finn shook his head. "But I expect us to reach Kelly's Island by nightfall, which is a good thing. The darkness will help shroud us. We'll anchor some ways out and row ashore quietly. Let's just hope there's no one guarding the beach we roll up on."

\*\*\*

The night sky fell upon us as we neared Kelly's Island, the full moon glowing like a spotlight while we descended the rope ladder to the rowboat below. Lottie stayed behind with Charlie as Gus, Finn, and myself rowed ashore. We had one thing on our side; Peter Easton's headquarters was located on the eastern shore and were coming in from the North.

"Remember what I told ye," Finn whispered. "Stay in the middle, always."

"I have no problem defending myself," I assured him which elicited a grunt from Gus behind me. "Well, I *can*."

"Yes, I'm sure," Gus spoke sarcastically as he rowed the ores. "The pretty cook from the future with no experience fightin'. Why don't we just let you lead the way?"

I kept my eyes on the beach in the distance and muttered under my breath, "shut up."

The boat rocked back as the bow hit bottom and we all jumped over to haul it onto the beach. A quick look around told us that no one was visibly watching the sandy stretch, but a thick wall of dense evergreens lined the island just a few meters in. The trees could be full of waiting attackers.

"Alright," Finn whispered as we huddled together. "Hands on yer weapon at all times, ready to draw. Ears open. Eyes searchin'." He took a few steps toward the forest and motioned over his shoulder for us to follow.

Gus's brow furrowed as he waited for me to move first so I stomped off after Finn. We entered the woods quietly, careful with every step. My heart raced with excitement, from the possibility of getting caught and also at the idea that I'd have Henry in my arms so soon. Oh, how they ached to hold him, touch him, and know that he was safe. Wicked thoughts of what Maria may be doing to him flickered across my mind and made my stomach toil. But I used it as fuel to keep going.

My reason for everything.

We climbed over foothills, sloshed across shallow creeks, all the while keeping the sound of the ocean waves crashing against the rocky shore of Kelly's Island within listening range. As long as the water kept to our left, we were heading in the right direction. A few times Finn turned to shush us and made us drop to the ground or behind a jagged boulder. He must have heard things I couldn't, but I trusted the Scot with my life and if he said get down, I got down. No questions asked.

Finally, the hint of firelight sparkled through the trees and my heart skipped a beat. We moved closer but kept a safe holding behind a massive uprooted tree, peeking our heads out to catch a better look at the beachfront house nestled in a tiny cove. It was surprisingly large for a secret headquarters, but not well built. A slightly leaning structure made of unfinished wood that had been greyed from the ocean's force stood near the beach. Three small outbuildings, sheds really, could be found off to the side. The main house glowed from the inside with candlelight and a raging bonfire burned just outside on the sand. Gus pulled out a small telescope from inside his coat and held it up to his eye.

"I don't see anyone at all," he informed us. "No movement in the windows, either."

I took a step forward, but Finn's arm shot out in front of me. "Where do ye think yer goin'?"

"To rescue Henry, isn't that why we came all this way?"

"For a time traveler ye sure ain't smart," he replied.

"We can't just go storming in there," Gus said, his voice low. "It looks quiet now, but we could be outnumbered once inside. And who knows what's in those other buildings."

I shrugged in defeat. "Then what do we do?"

"We stay right here and suss out the situation," Gus told me. "Keep looking. We just need an idea of how many people Maria has with her."

I didn't like that idea. The thought of Henry possibly being just a few yards away killed me. I kept it calm on the outside, but every fiber of my being was screaming from the inside, demanding that I obey and just *go*. I stood and waited patiently, but the second their attention wasn't on me, I took off.

"Dianna!" Finn called, and I heard Gus cover his mouth as the end of my name became muffled.

I could hear their footsteps close behind me, but I never faltered, just kept scaling down the jagged hillside of the forest's edge toward the beach. I stole a quick glance over my shoulder and saw the two of them trailing me. I pushed myself as hard as I could, forced my legs to move just a little faster, my arms to pump a little stronger.

I just had to outrun them. I could slip inside, stay hidden, and search every room until I found Henry. Sure, there was a good chance I'd get caught. But it was a risk I was willing to make. I couldn't stand the thought of Maria's hands on Henry for a second longer. My lungs burned and threatened to betray me. I slipped into the shadows of the side of the building and bent over to catch my breath, but it only took a few seconds for Finn and Gus to get there.

"What the Christ are ye doin', ye crazy wench?" Finn whispered angrily as he grabbed my arm, his breaths huffing and strained from running.

I yanked it away. "I'm here to save the man I love. Not stand around in the trees waiting to see if he's even here." The two still looked angry but said nothing. "Now are you with me or not?"

I pointed to a low window just a few feet away and motioned for them to follow. We crept alongside the building and snuggled up to the opening. I slowly peeked around the frame to look inside and found the main floor when you first enter to be empty of people. I nodded to the two of my companions and we carefully made our way over to the next one. Again, I peered inside and gasped at the sight waiting there.

A tall, broad figure sat in a chair, slumped over and tied with ropes. His back was to the window, so we couldn't see his face, but I didn't need to. I'd know the shape of Henry even if I were blind. His every feature marked into my brain like a roadmap. I stared in awe, frozen, unable to tear my eyes away as I watched his shoulders slowly heave with every breath.

"That's him," I choked out and touched my hand to the glass pane. "He's right there."

Finn peered in next to my head. "I'll be damned, so he is."

"There's no one around," I whispered. "Maybe they're gone off to get supplies or something?"

"Or it could be a trap," Gus muttered.

I shrugged. "How would they even know to set one? No one knew we were coming."

"The Cobhams have their ways," the grumpy pirate replied, and Finn nodded in agreement. "They have eyes and ears everywhere."

I blew out an impatient huff of air and peeked in the window again, worried that he would just disappear. I was desperate. I needed to get to him. My eyes scanned the edges of the old-fashioned window and realized it could be raised from the outside. I applied a little pressure and pushed upwards, stopping when the ancient frame made a loud creaking sound.

"What are ye doin'?" Finn whispered frantically.

"This is a closed room. No one's inside. I can slip in, untie him, and we'd slip back out before anyone even noticed he was missing."

The two looked hesitant but didn't argue. I took

that as a yes and continued to shimmy the window open enough for my body to fit. Finally, I poked one leg in and carefully slipped my body through the opening.

When both my feet quietly hit the floor of the dark room, I turned and gave them a thumb's up. I slowly tip-toed over to the figure in the chair and, in the dim light of a single candle, realized there was a fabric bag over his hanging head. Hesitantly, fingers trembling, I grabbed hold and yanked it off.

My heart pounded from the inside of my chest, nearly knocking the breath from my body at the startling sight of him. My beautiful Henry, beaten and bloody, his face swollen, mouth cracked and dried. He was slumped over, a lifeless body straining against the ropes that bound his torso to the chair. I didn't want to think it, but he looked... dead. My lips juddered as I fought back tears and reached a hand out to caress his bloodied face. He suddenly came to life and began to resist my touch, the chair bouncing and making a racket as he struggled against my presence.

"Don't touch me—"

I slipped my hand over his mouth and shushed him, praying that no one heard us. "Henry, it's *me*," I spoke softly, and his convulsing body came to a halt. His eyes were both swollen shut, but his face twisted into a mixture of pain and disbelief.

"D-Dianna?"

The sound of my broken name across his trembling lips was enough to shatter me. I threw my arms around his limp body and held him so tight he winced from the pain. But I felt his frame strain against the ropes, reaching out to me in desperation.

"Yes, it's me, baby, it's me," I assured him and held his face in my hands before placing a warm kiss on his coarse lips. Our hot tears mixed together, and Henry's mouth held on to mine like a starved vampire tasting blood once again.

"Untie me," he demanded, "before I lose my damn mind."

I stood and walked behind the chair to loosen the ties but found a massive heap of knots that I could never undo in time. So, I unsheathed my trusty dagger from my side and sliced through the ropes, letting them fall and pool around the legs of the chair. I then did the same for the bloodstained twine that bound my beloved's wrists. His hands immediately reached out for me and I kneeled down to ease myself into his embrace, weary of the fact he couldn't see through the giant, swollen lumps around his eyes. It didn't stop his tears from pouring down, though.

"My God," he whispered shakily, mauling my curls as he did. A delusional laugh erupting from his throat. "This must be a dream. I never thought I'd taste your lips again." His unsteady hand caressed my cheek, trailing down my neck and he sobbed. "Or touch your precious skin." The man held me close and kissed my mouth before pulling back. "I only wish I could see your face."

I carefully touched my fingers to his puffy eyes. "Jesus... what did she do to you?"

His hands ran through my thick hair and pulled me in again, his mouth moving against mine as he spoke. Dry and trembling. "Nothing as painful as my crying heart. God, Dianna, I thought I'd never see you again."

My chest erupted with heaving sobs at the broken man I held within my arms. "I'm so sorry."

"Shhh, don't be," he whispered in my ear. "It's not your fault, none of it is."

"Uh, I hate to break up the heartfelt reunion," Finn whispered loudly through the window, "But we best be on our way."

"Finnigan?" Henry perked up and turned toward the sound of his friend's voice.

"Aye, captain, and Gus, too."

"Can you walk?" I asked him.

"Of course," he replied with a raspy growl and then stubbornly attempted to stand on two feet.

When I felt him waver, I slipped my shoulder under his arm and led him to the window where Gus and Finn helped him out.

Immediately, Finn grabbed Henry. "Aye, Christ, it's good to see ye, captain."

Henry returned a gruff pat on the back with a weak attempt. "You, as well, old friend. You as well." He turned then, searching. "Augustus?"

"Right here, captain," Gus chimed in and stepped toward Henry. He appeared solemn. "Henry, I—"

"Don't," Henry waved a hand, "not now. Let's get

out of here. I haven't heard a sound in the house for hours. They're bound to be back any moment."

"How many of them are there?" Finn asked.

"Just Eric and Maria," he replied and fought through a sudden fit of coughing, spitting blood on the ground at his feet. "She's gone... mad. Refuses to trust anyone. They haven't a crew, even."

"That's good," Gus said. "Come on, I'll lead the way across the beach. We have to hurry."

I let Henry's arm fall heavy over my shoulders while Finn grabbed the other and we slipped out from the shadows of the house. With a quick look around, we took off in a line across the front yard and around the fire pit. Suddenly, the blaze burst into a massive flame and the sound of wet glass breaking rang in my ears. We stopped to look back and I saw the shape of two figures standing on the front porch.

"Look what you made me do. Wasted a perfectly good bottle of rum." She paused to cluck her tongue. "Where the *Hell* do you think you're taking my pet?"

The sound of her voice awoke something deep inside, something dark and angry, but also a memory. A reminder of the wound, still not fully healed, that she'd left on my body. Gus and Finn drew their swords and I slipped my dagger out with my free hand, shifting my body to somewhat shield Henry.

"He's not your pet, Maria," I called out. "I told you before. Henry is *mine*. I'm just here to take him back."

Maria Cobham stepped down onto the sand, her clunky leather boot buckles jingling with every brazen step she took toward us. Soon, she was close enough for the light of the fire to catch her face, highlighting the stark contrast of black curls against her pallor skin. Big, brown eyes glared into mine, like an evil doppelganger staring at me from a mirror's reflection. I hadn't paid enough attention last time, to really see how our resemblance was far too uncanny. Sure, there were slight differences; her hair was wilder, her face worn from years of piracy. But Maria Cobham was like a sick and twisted version of myself. No wonder everyone thought I was her.

"Oh, is that so?" she quipped and jutted her jaw back and forth like a crack addict would. "Tell her, pet. Tell her how you wanted to come with me. Tell her how you begged me to take you."

My eyes shot to Henry and, even though he couldn't see the hint betrayal on my face, I could see the torment on his. "No, Dianna, I swear, it wasn't as she says."

"You evil, bitch!" Gus held his sword out and lunged toward the villainess, but she stepped back and pulled out a pistol, aiming straight for him.

"*Tell* her, pet," Maria insisted and, when Henry didn't obey, she clicked the hammer and held it in place.

"Alright!" he yelled at her.

"Henry?" I spoke with sadness and disbelief. "It's

not true, is it? Why would you give yourself back to her like that?"

"He did it to save me, Dianna," Gus called over from a few feet away. "He offered himself willingly if she let me live that night in the forest. She tied me up, so I wouldn't follow."

I looked at Maria, eyes narrowed. But it all made sense now. The Cobhams were notorious throughout history for never leaving a soul behind. And I know Henry would never have gone down without a fight. Without dying first.

"You're scum," I spat at her.

The mouth of the pistol then turned and aimed at me and Maria's face twisted into a sick grin. "If I'm scum then so are you, blood-kin." My heart beat wildly as she took a step closer. "It's too bad poor Henry can't see it when I bleed the life from your body. Just one little flick of a finger and *bang*, you're gone." I could see the workings of a plan forming in her mind. "Maybe I should take you with us, wait until my pet's eyes open. He shouldn't miss it. I could even take back my jacket, you thief."

Just then, her husband Eric jumped down from the front porch and sidled up next to her. He was a tall man, just a few inches more than she with a stern, expressionless face. She looked over her shoulder at him and smiled. "Looks like we're going to have some company on our trip, after all."

But, to everyone's shock, when Maria Cobham returned her gaze to on us, her husband hauled back and laid a blow to her head with a chunk of driftwood. Her pistol went off and shot far in the distance. The sound deafening to my ears. I stared in disbelief as her body went limp and folded over, falling to the sand.

"What the bloody Christ?" Finn sputtered.

Eric dropped the piece of wood, his face deadpan as he glanced at us and heaved a deep sigh. "Get out of here while you can."

We wavered, unsure.

"Go!" he screamed at us.

We turned and bolted across the beach, through the forest, heading back the way we came. Neither of us spoke, the rhythm of our labored breaths the only sound to be heard aside from the crisp cracking of the forest floor beneath our steady feet. We halted, briefly, a few times for a very weak Henry to catch his breath, but we soon found ourselves on the Northern beach of Kelly's Island and piled into the little rowboat we came in.

Henry sat on the floor in the middle and I slipped in, propping his body up in my arms. I noticed that he'd gone limp, what little energy he'd had left behind in a mixture of adrenaline across the forest. He passed out and I held him tightly, looking up at the stars and thanking the heavens that I was able to do it. That I had the strength and persistence to save him. I began to cry as the adrenaline seeped from my body, uncontrollable ugly sobs of happiness as Gus and Finn frantically rowed us back to our new home aboard The Queen.

# CHAPTER THIRTEEN

After we tiredly hauled Henry's wilted body up the side of our ship and scrambled aboard, Lottie came scurrying out to meet us.

"You're back!" she exclaimed. I tried to ignore the sense of utter surprise dipped in her voice. She glanced down at Henry's massive body sprawled out on the deck's floor and took in the state of his injuries. "My God, you did it."

"Barely," I told her. "But, yes, we did it. Can you get me some clean cloth and a pan of warm soapy water?"

"Of course," Lottie replied but hesitated. "Are you guys alright?" I noticed her eyes flicker to Gus. "Are any of you hurt?"

"Nay," Finn grunted and stuck out his chest

proudly. "Our fearless leader here led us right to him, didn't think twice about bargin' right into Maria Cobham's hideout."

I rolled my eyes but couldn't help the tiny smile that found its way to my lips as I turned and bent down next to Henry. "Help me get him in my quarters."

We carried Henry inside, over to my bed, and he still didn't wake. I began to worry that his injuries, as gruesome as they appeared, were far worse than we thought. What if he fell into a coma and never woke up? What if he suffered brain trauma from the beatings and was bleeding on the brain as we stood there and watched over him? I shook the morbid thoughts away and tried to keep it together. No, he would be fine. I didn't make it that far only to lose him. Not when I finally had him in my grasp.

"Thank you, guys," I told Gus and Finn.

"Of course, captain," Finn happily replied. "It was my honor."

"And you say that with actual sincerity," I quipped. My eyes fell to Gus.

He was quiet, thoughtful. Then he inhaled deeply. "You're going to make a fine captain, Dianna." I brightened at the compliment, but he added, "you've got a bloody lot to learn. But I'm pleased to help ya along the way."

"Thanks," I sat down on the bed next to Henry, "but he's the real captain, we'll do it together."

Lottie returned with washcloths and a pan of

warm water in hand. "Here you go," she said and laid it down on the floor by my feet.

"Thanks, Lottie," I told her warmly. "How's Charlie doing?"

She stood and smiled. "He's great. Still can't speak, but we're gettin' along just fine. I already told him you're back. The poor boy, I could just see the relief push him down into his bed."

I nodded. "Good." Then looked to my sailing master. "Finn set a course to... anywhere. Just get us out of here and as far away as possible so we can hide away until Henry and Charlie are fully healed."

"Aye, captain," he replied and tipped his head before leaving. Gus and Lottie filed out after him with a wave.

The door closed behind them and I walked over to lock it. I pressed my back against it and let everything wash over me. All the fear and anxiety I'd been storing up inside flooded from my limbs and I tipped my head back in peace. It was over. All of it. Just days ago, I'd been sitting on my bed in Rocky Harbour, crying over the loss of the life I had left behind in the past. But I traveled back through time, found my friends, made new ones, secured a ship of my very own, and managed to rescue my beloved from the grips of an evil psychopath. All the while, carrying the life of a child inside me.

I was exhausted, but I felt indestructible.

I removed my boots and jacket, then hung them on the beautiful red chair before tending to Henry.

With a knife, I cut away his tattered clothes and threw them on the floor, leaving a naked man laying there on my quilted blanket. It was then that I could truly see the extent of his injuries. His massive frame was peppered with a rainbow of bruises, his chest covered in burns and incisions. I couldn't believe my eyes. Along with his beaten and swollen face, Henry looked like someone who'd been dragged off a battlefield.

I soaked a cloth in the warm, soapy water and wrung it out. Carefully, I washed the sweat, dirt, and blood from his body, mesmerized by the broken beauty that was this man. I would take him in any form. I worked until the pan of water turned a solid color of deep crimson and then covered his naked body with a fresh blanket, giving the wounds a chance to air out. I then slipped off my own clothes and slid under the blanket with Henry, our warm bodies melding together as I wrapped my tired arms around him. I soon drifted into a deep, comfortable sleep and I only prayed that's where Henry was, too.

***

I knew I was dreaming. The vague sense of surroundings covered me in a blurry cloud, but one thing was certain. Henry was there. I lay on my back, the soft warm sand brushing up against my skin, and looked up at him in admiration. The sun shone from behind his head, creating a halo of light around his beautiful blonde hair and I reached up to touch his flawless face. A face free of the bloody wounds I knew I'd just cleaned.

"I missed you," I told him.

He leaned in and took my mouth in his, a passionate kiss so full of emotion I could feel it plunging deep into my gut. He pulled away and smiled. I could feel the tendons of the dream loosening and slipping away, alerting me to the fact that I was waking up and I scrambled after him, desperate.

I awoke with a gasp like I'd been thrown back into my body and immediately searched for Henry but succumbed to the heavy sense of relief at the sight of him sleeping soundly next to me. The sun was up, and it filled the room with a golden hue. I had to remind myself to relax, that it was all over. I sunk back down and nestled up next to the beautiful pirate, basking in the warmth of his massive body.

I felt him shift and open his dry mouth. He moaned, deep and hoarse as he returned my embrace, our nakedness colliding. "What a mighty pleasant way to wake up." His scruffy chin scratched the top of my hair and I heard him inhale deeply. "I never thought I'd smell the sweet scent of you again."

"Good morning," I replied and kissed his chest. "We'll never have to spend another morning apart. I swear it."

"Nothing would make me happier," he replied.

"Except, perhaps, a glass of water."

I laughed and carefully crawled over Henry to fetch him something to drink from the table. I helped him sit up and held the mouth of the glass to his lips as he drank. When he was finished, his hands reached out for me, blindly, as his eyes were still swollen shut. But I could see movement around the slits as his face shifted with expressions. A good sign.

"I would kill someone for the ability to feast my eyes on your naked body," he told me with a raspy growl. Goosebumps scoured down across my skin at the sound, a sound I'd missed so much.

I grabbed his wrists and held the palms to my breasts. "You don't need eyes to see me, Henry."

His hands slid down and grabbed me by the waist, then pulled me on top of him with ease. Even in his weak and wounded state, my burly pirate king had no problem taking what was his.

I leaned down and kissed him, then smiled. It was time to share the news that I'd been protecting for so long. "Henry," I whispered excitedly. "I have a surprise for you."

I felt his calloused fingers caressing the skin of my back. "There's no better gift than the one I hold right here, Dianna, my savior."

I reached behind and took his hands in mine, guiding them to my front and turning his palms to face my belly, pressing them there. "Are you sure?"

He appeared confused at first and then I could see the pieces of the puzzle slowly fall into place in his mind. I'm sure if his eyes could open they'd be sparkling, for tears poured from them, regardless. "You're with child?"

I beamed. "Yes."

"We're... we're going to have a baby?" His words were strained behind the tears.

I leaned down and kissed his face, touched my lips to the wetness of his cheeks. "Yes, Henry. You're going to be a father."

He shot up from the bed and grabbed my hips, flipping me over on my back and hovered above. "How did the heavens see fit to make me so lucky?"

"Luck has nothing to do with it," I assured him and ran my fingers through his straggly blonde hair. I'd missed those golden locks and I prayed our child inherited them. His face turned and cupped his mouth in my palm, placing a long and gentle kiss there. Suddenly, his arms began to shake, and his head swayed.

"Are you alright?" His left arm buckled, and he collapsed at my side. "Jesus, Henry!"

"I'm fine, just dizzy. I haven't eaten in days."

I propped myself up to examine him. "And the blood loss, I imagine." I stuck a leg over his torso to crawl out of bed. "I'll get you some food."

His trembling fingers grabbed hold of my thighs. "Wait, I'm dizzy not dying, woman." Henry situated me across his hips, so my legs straddled his sides and I could feel the warmth of his erection growing underneath me. "I may not have the strength to hold myself up, but I will always possess the ability to make love to you, Dianna."

I felt his forehead for fever. There was none. "Are you sure? Maybe we should eat first?"

"I'll feast on the divine beast before me and have my fill," he replied, driving his hips upward.

I couldn't help but grin and leaned over to touch my lips to his, breathing in the scent of this glorious man, and tightening my grip on those driving hips. "Lay back and relax, sailor. I'll take over from here."

\*\*\*

I walked the length of The Queen, taking in the beauty of my ship in the crisp mid-morning sun. Finn stood at the wheel as he monitored the crew. I headed over to say good morning.

"More like good afternoon," he replied and threw me a wink. "the day's half gone, captain."

I laughed. "Can you do me a favor?"

"Of course, anythin'."

"Can you fetch me a pail of seawater?"

His brow creased. "Sure. For what?"

"It's the coldest thing I can get aboard the ship for Henry's face, and the salt should help reduce the swelling, too."

"Aye, ye and yer magic," he replied cheekily.

I laughed again and turn to leave. The young deckhands that Gus hired worked away, checking the sails, hauling ropes, and swabbing areas of the deck. They paused and smiled at me as I passed. I tried not to react bashfully when they greeted me as captain. It was a title I was determined to get used to.

I found the ladder and made my way down to the lower deck where the heavy aroma of breakfast still hung in the air. The mess deck was so much bigger than the one we had aboard The Devil's Heart and I felt bad that we didn't have the crew to fill it. But I had to remind myself that we had all we needed. Keep our circle small and our problems smaller. I easily found the kitchen and entered through the swinging doors to a startled Lottie and Gus. They'd been standing quite close to one another and quickly broke away with my arrival.

I pretended to see nothing out of the ordinary. "Is there any breakfast left?"

"Good morning, captain," Lottie replied, her cheeks flushed with blood. "Um, yes. We had eggs and toast. I can prepare a tray and bring it up to you if you like."

I tipped my head and arched an eyebrow. "Lottie, please, just call me Dianna. This is ridiculous."

"Um, alright, if you're sure," she replied.

"Yes, God, yes." Then, with a second thought, I added, "I mean, maybe not in front of the new deckhands. But otherwise, I'm Dianna. We're friends. Please."

"You have no worries about them boys, captain," Gus chimed in. "I scooped them up young for a reason. They're more trustworthy than an old sea dog. They'll be loyal, through and through. I'll see to it."

I smiled and nodded. "I have no doubt."

An awkward silence made its way around the room and I could tell Gus wasn't sure if he should leave or not.

"Um, Lottie, you can just throw everything on a tray and I can take it back with me," I told her.

"Oh, sure." She began to scuttle around like a busy bee. I'd never seen her so nervous.

Gus stepped closer. "How's he doing today?"

"Much better. I cleaned his wounds the best I could. They don't look infected, so that's a bonus. He just needs time to heal and regain his strength. Apparently, he hasn't eaten in days."

"Henry's strong," Gus said. "I've never seen anyone built like him in my life."

"I know." I shook my head in awe. "What he's been through, not just recently but in his life, that woman..." It made me sick to even think the horrid thoughts.

Gus nodded in agreement, knowing exactly what I tried to convey. "He should be all kinds of messed up, shouldn't he?"

"Yeah, but he's not. How can that be?"

"He was headin' down that road," Gus informed me. "I saw it. Every day, he retreated further and further into the dark room in his mind." He inhaled deeply and leaned against the counter. "Then you came in like the wind and blew the door open. Made him smile. Made him feel loved. It's a good thing."

"Aww Gus, you ol' softie," I patted his arm, "you can have that, too, you know?" I made eyes in Lottie's direction over by the stove and laughed at how I made the otherwise grumpy pirate blush.

Lottie came over to us then, tray in hand. "Here you go. The eggs are cold, but the tea is hot."

I took the heavy tray and thanked her, giving Gus a cheeky wink before heading back up to my quarters. I grabbed the small bucket of freezing sea water from Finn along the way, looping the handle over my arm as I juggled everything. I had to set the tray down on the deck outside my door so I could turn the knob, but I was soon in the quiet of my quarters and alone with Henry.

He stirred in the bed and turned to face me. "Dianna?"

"Yes, it's me," I told him and dipped a fresh cloth in the ice water. "I've got something to help your face."

"Is it your warm bosom?" he joked.

I let a grin spread across my face. God, I had missed him so much. I still couldn't believe I had him back.

"You wish," I kidded. "Now, lay back. It's going to be cold, but it'll speed up the healing process and bring down your swelling. If it works, you should be able to open your eyes soon." I laid the cold, salted cloth across his puffy eyes and he tried to stifle a wince. "Sorry, the salt in the water is going to sting your wounds a little."

I rested my bottom on the edge of the bed and

gently scratched his golden scruff with my fingertips. I missed the feel of it. Henry turned his face toward my palm and kissed it, sending goosebumps trailing up my arm. It still felt surreal, that he was even there. Alive and in my bed.

"How is everyone?" he asked.

"Good," I replied and checked the cloth. It had already lost most of its chill, so I wrung it out in the ice water again. "We have a small crew, but enough to keep us sailing. Finn said he's steering us to a small inlet over near Cupers Cove so we can lie low for a while. We've got plenty of food and supplies."

"You're quite the captain," Henry told me with a sly grin.

"Hardly," I replied and grabbed a plate of scrambled eggs. "Here, open up." I fed him a few bites and listened to his moans of delight at the taste of food on his tongue. "I can't believe she was starving you."

"Dianna, listen to me," Henry said, a serious tone carrying his words. "I don't want you to worry about what may or may not have been done to me. It's over. You saved me, in more ways than I can count. There is nothing that woman can do to me, now or ever, that would be worse than the thought of losing you. I see that now."

"What do you mean?"

"When I watched you tear through the threads of time and disappear before my eyes, a part of me died." I caught his swollen and cracked bottom lip tremble as he spoke, and I wanted to cry. "She beat me, day after day. Tried to pry information from my mind through starvation, taunting, threats. But I could endure it all. No matter what she did, it could never reach that dead part of my soul."

I was almost afraid to ask, but I did. "What... what information was she prying for?"

He sighed thoughtfully. "Give me some more of those eggs, would you?"

"Henry."

His expression morphed into a frown. "Dianna, think about it. We all witnessed what happened to you."

I thought for a second. Then the answer came to life and unfolded in my mind. I knew then what he meant. "She was trying to figure out who I am, wasn't she?"

"Yes," he replied reluctantly, then added before opening his mouth, "Eggs, please."

"What did you tell her?"

"This cloth is warm again," he said, trying to distract me.

I let out an exaggerated sigh, soaked it in the ice water and wrung it out before placing it back over his eyes. "*Tell* me. Should I be concerned?"

Henry sat up, the cloth falling from his face, and he felt for my hands. "I would never let any harm come to you, Dianna. Do you understand? I would protect you and our child with my body and my life before I ever let Maria Cobham lay a hand on you."

I chewed on my bottom lip. "That sounds like I

should be concerned." Henry squeezed my hands and I could sense his worry. "Shit. What did you tell her?"

"Nothing at first," he replied. "But then… she manipulated the information from me. I didn't even understand what it was she was after until it was too late. I was just trying to protect your honor—"

"Henry! My God, just tell me!" My worry quickly grew to fear, and I suddenly knew we weren't safe like I'd thought. We never would be as long as she roamed the same Earth as us.

"Dianna," Henry spoke softly, carefully. "How much do you know about your mother?"

I tried to hide the shock I felt at the mention of my mom. What did she have to do with any of it?

"I don't know," I shrugged and searched my brain for answers, "she was from the past, she time travelled by accident like I did, only she went to the future and met my dad. They fell in love and had me. She decided to stay in the future with us and then drowned when I was in my teens."

"How did you find out this information?" he asked.

I felt more and more uneasy and my words became a whisper. "Her journal."

"Did it happen to mention what year she came to the future from?"

I thought for a moment. "No, it didn't. Why? Henry, what the Hell is going on?"

"Please don't be upset with me, but I don't think

your mother drowned, Dianna."

Tears welled in my eyes and my throat went dry. "W-what? How can you say that?"

"I have reason to believe she may have come to your father from sometime in the late 1600s and that she went back, she'd found a way."

I stood up from the bed, head shaking in disbelief. But I couldn't help but remember how I'd gotten back to the past myself. If I didn't leave a note for Aunt Mary, my disappearance would have looked like a drowning.

"No, *no*...why would you think that? What did Maria tell you?"

Tears streamed down my face then. My mother's death and disappearance was something I'd put to rest years ago. But talking about her like this... it was like the pain from a fresh wound.

"Because when I finally spoke your name she went mad, more than her usual insane self," Henry told me, his sightless face following the sound of my pacing footsteps around the room. "And afterward, she lost all interest in me. She became obsessed with this new plan. Details, maps, gathering supplies for a long trip. I could tell Eric was growing tired of her."

"Where was she going?"

"Back to England," he replied, a strange sadness in his tone, "to find and kill her mother, a woman who Maria claimed never truly loved her. I'd heard rumors over the years that Maria's mother was a cold woman, was partly to blame for the path of darkness Maria had been pushed down." He paused and patted the blanket next to him. "Dianna, come and sit, please."

"Who's her mother? What does that have to do with me and *my* mother?"

"Dianna—"

"Henry!" I shrieked, hot tears of desperation pouring down my face. I was sure I already knew the answer, but I needed him to say it. I needed to hear it for the words to ring true.

"Maria's mother's name was... *is* Constance Cobham."

I began to back away, mouth gaping as a silent cry choked from my body.

"Maria Cobham isn't your ancestor," Henry continued. His words like nails in my coffin. "She's your sister."

# CHAPTER FOURTEEN

A while later, we sat on the cold floor of my quarters, Henry's long arms wrapped around me consolingly. I'd thrown a world class fit upon learning the news of mine and Maria's true connection. The reason why we looked so similar. The sense of recognition I felt in her presence.

She was my sister.

But I'd processed that information much faster than the second realization Henry bestowed upon me. My mom wasn't dead. All this time, she hadn't drowned in the sea by our home in Rocky Harbour. No, she'd used the lore of magic to call the siren and go back to where she came from. She willingly left me. But even that wasn't the part I struggled so hard with.

My sweet, caring, loving mother raised Maria, the

scourge of the earth. She could very well have been the reason Maria Cobham became what she is and a part of me simply couldn't believe it. There had to be more to the story. I had to get to the bottom of it.

"I'm sorry," I muttered and wiped the snotty tears from my face as I pried my cheek off Henry's bare chest.

"You have nothing to be sorry for, Dianna," he assured me. "And, honestly, I'm not sure how I didn't piece it together myself. I knew Maria's mother's name this whole time, but my mind never connected the dots."

I wrapped the wool blanket around my shoulders as I stood and then helped Henry to his feet, noting that he was still stark naked. "Don't you dare."

"What?"

"Try to make this your fault," I told him. "It's not."

"Alright," the man accepted, "so what do you propose we do now?"

"Well," I replied and smirked, licking my tear stained lips, taking in the glorious figure before me, "we should probably start with getting you some clothes." I opened the wardrobe I'd filled with clothing for both of us and pulled out a few garments. "Then, is it..."

Henry waited for me to finish and when I didn't, he spoke, "What? Tell me what you want to do, Dianna. I'll see that it happens."

"Is it possible for us to go to England?"

I slipped the white blouse over his head and helped feed his arms through the sleeves.

"It is, yes." Next, his trousers. "Are you suggesting what I think you're suggesting?"

I thought for a moment, assessing the idea.

"Yes," I finally spoke. "I want to sail to England after Maria and save my mother. If she hasn't left yet, she's sure to leave soon, right?" I inhaled deeply. "Is it a crazy idea?"

Henry took me in his arms, the swelling of his face gone down enough for me to see the expression of sheer admiration. "All the best ones are."

I laughed and brought my lips to his, standing on my toes to do so. I felt as if there were nothing I couldn't do with Henry by my side. "I love you so much."

"And I you, Time Traveller." His hands raked through my hair as his body pressed against me, wanting. "My Pirate Queen."

"Mmm, I like the sound of that." I kissed him again and then touched the puffy skin around his eyes. "The swelling is going down fast, you should be able to see again any day now. Just keep putting the cold water on it."

He feigned a frown. "The salt water burns."

"Don't be a baby," I told him jokingly.

Henry then dropped to one knee and placed a kiss on my stomach. "Yes, a baby, indeed." He hugged me tight to his face. "My everything right here in my hands." We remained there, him nuzzling my belly, me curling my fingers in his hair until he spoke again. "There's one problem with your idea, Dianna."

"What's that?" I asked as he brought himself to his feet.

"That's a Hell of a journey. We'd need supplies, and money to get them."

I chewed on my bottom lip. "I've spent just about all I have, aside from a few schillings. How much are we talking about here?"

"Well, we'd have to verify with Finnigan, but it would surely be a three-month trip, especially this time of year. Food and supplies for all eight of us, as well as the livestock..." he paused, contemplating, "Well, let's just say I wish I had that treasure chest we found together."

I slumped down in my red velvet chair and rocked back and forth, lost in thought. It was a crazy idea. A three-month journey across the Atlantic with just eight people and a pregnant captain. It was a recipe for disaster, even if we could afford it. My eyes scanned the room and landed on the long bookshelf near the old sofa. Suddenly, an idea dawned on me and I dove for the books.

"What is it, what are you doing?" Henry asked me.

I began pulling the leather-bound wonders from the shelf, searching for the captain's logs. "If Lottie's father and grandfather were connected to Peter Easton, then surely there would be evidence of where he hid his treasures."

"Treasures?"

"Yes, in my time, there are so many stories of Easton's escapades. He raided the Atlantic for years and is believed to be one of the wealthiest pirates that ever lived." I flipped feverishly through pages. "But one story sticks out in my mind more than others. Near the end of his reign, the Spanish sent a fleet to come to Newfoundland and arrest him. But Easton fled with three chests of treasure. He entrusted two men from his crew to hide it over near Corner Brook," I strained to remember the exact place, "um, Shell Bird Island, I think?"

Henry felt for the chair and sat down with a cold, salt water cloth and leaned back to cover his eyes. "Go on, I'm listening."

"Well, the story says that one of the men shot the other and buried him with the chests. Then he drowned on the way back to his captain. Leaving the exact location of the treasure a mystery, even to Peter Easton himself."

"Well, that would drive any man insane," Henry quipped.

"Yeah, people have searched for years on and around Shell Bird Island, but no one's ever found it."

"Then how do we know it's true?" Henry asked as he reached over to soak his cloth in the cold water again.

"We don't," I replied with a grin. "But I know someone who might."

\*\*\*

Lottie sat across the desk from me, fiddling with the hem of her apron. I'd asked Finn to go get her for me and Henry left with him when she arrived, giving us some privacy but claiming to need fresh air.

"So, what's this all about, then?" she asked me.

I smiled at the sight of the diamond studs in her ears. "Do you like my gift?"

She absentmindedly reached up to touch one. "Yes, thank you. You don't have to give me anything, you know."

"I know," I assured her. "But I wanted to. It's a token of my friendship and appreciation for The Queen." I leaned back in my chair. "God, it's the least I could do for what you've given me."

"Is that what this is about?" she continued. "Did you need them back?"

"No! Goodness, no," I told my friend. "They're yours. Keep them." I stole a glance at the stack of captain's logs I'd been reading. "Lottie, you said you grew up on this ship, right?"

She looked nervous. "Yes, why?"

"I haven't told everyone yet, but we're going to be heading out on a really long journey."

She leaned back and crossed her arms. "How long? Where are we going?"

"England."

She bolted forward. "England? Jesus, Dianna, that's two or three months at sea before we even meet landfall."

"I know," I replied. "And we're going to need some serious money to fund a trip like that. Not to mention the means to survive once we're there, and then for the journey back."

Her big blue eyes stared at me. "So, what does this have to do with me?"

"Lottie, did your father ever mention The Treasure of Shell Bird Island?" Her look of shock was enough to tell me the answer.

"How do you—"

"I know all about it," I said. "And I also know that it's enough to fund a thousand trips to England."

"That treasure is cursed," she replied curtly.

"How so?" I amused.

I knew damn well it wasn't. But then a part of me wondered if that was possible. That maybe a curse is the reason no one's ever found it. Who was I to say magic and curses didn't exist?

"You have to travel through The Devil's Dancing Pools just to get to the mouth of the caves," she explained. "Cave's apparently protected by sirens. And then the treasure itself..." she shook her head and stood, turning away from me in frustration. "No, it's not possible. We'll all likely be killed."

"What about the treasure?"

"It's protected by a Watchman," Lottie told me.

I shrugged. "What's that?"

She ran her hands through her hair in exasperation as she paced the floor. "My grandfather was on that mission, you know?" She didn't wait for my reply, just kept pacing. "They said he drowned trying to get back to Easton's ship, but that was a lie. My grandfather shot and killed the poor bugger who was sent with him, then buried the body with the treasure."

I chewed on my lips as I listened. Then I realized. "A watchman."

Lottie nodded. "He abandoned his captain and fled back to England with the location of the treasure locked away in his mind." She finally stopped pacing and turned to face me. "But not before he told my father."

My eyes widened. "Your father? But he would have been just a boy."

"Yes, I know. His memory of it was foggy, but we spent years sailing back and forth to the West Coast, searching for the cave. It wasn't until the year he died that we finally figured it out."

"Figured what out?"

Lottie's eyes glossed over as they faded away in thought. "I was still just a girl, barely sixteen. We figured it out together one night after looking at maps for hours. But he refused to take me." She came over to my desk then and rolled out one of the maps that sat atop of it, pointing to the area over near Corner Brook. "See, here is where everyone knows Shell Bird Island to be." Her finger skimmed across the paper, coming closer to where we currently were and stopping at a minuscule dot. "But here, nestled right in this cove just off the South East Coast is Shellbed Isle. And if you mispronounce it?"

I beamed. "Shell Bird Island."

"Exactly, and look," she pointed to the spot just before it, a long and narrow inlet. "The Devil's Dancing Pools."

I stared at the map unblinkingly. "Rapids. Of course. If you can get through the rapids, you'd come to a pool of calm water, which is probably where the mouth of the cave is." Excitement flowed through my veins. We were going to get that treasure. But then one look at Lottie and all of that came to a halt. "But, wait. Your father. You said he went?"

"Yes, he went." Her eyes glistened with tears again. "And he never came back."

I stood on my side of the desk and reached a hand over to cover hers. "I'm so sorry."

Lottie sniffled and wiped away a stray tear. "It's fine, it was a long time ago."

For a moment, I wanted to toss the whole idea. But I was determined. I had a mission and that treasure was the key to everything. I shifted my hand from hers and planted my fingers on Shellbed Isle. "We're going."

"What?" she replied in disbelief.

"We'll make it," I assured her. "I've been white water rafting dozens of times. I can maneuver us through the dancing pools."

Lottie backed away, shaking her head in confusion. "Whitewater–" she paused and her face turned to anger. "But what about the sirens and the Watchman?"

"I have a feeling we can get past the sirens," I told her, thinking of my own encounter and hoping it would work in my favor again. "And we'll have three burly pirates with us. I think we can handle a single ghostly guard." She seemed to vibrate with anger or fear, I wasn't sure which one, as she considered my words. A few moments passed before either of spoke again.

"Why?" she finally asked. "Why are we suddenly going to England? Why all the urgency?"

I inhaled deeply. This was a moment of truth. I had to come clean about it all if I honestly valued the new friendship Lottie had given me. "Sit back down," I told her, and she did. "I have something to tell you."

\*\*\*

Finn, Gus, Henry, Lottie, and I all stood around my desk as I told them the plan. Lottie was silent, distant, only nodding now and then to remain in on the conversation. But her eyes kept glancing in my direction, wondering, disbelieving.

"I said it, didnae I," Finn exclaimed as he playfully punched Gus in the arm. Gus just rolled his eyes and sighed. "When we dragged her aboard the boat that day. The scraggly little thing."

"What do you mean?' I asked.

"First, I thought ye *were* Maria Cobham," Finn began, "Then I saw yer face and thought maybe ye were her sister. And what did ye say, Gus?"

The other pirate looked annoyed with his Scottish friend. "I don't know, something to the tune of... if Maria Cobham had a sister, she would have killed her years ago."

My stomach flopped at the vague memory. I feared for my life that day. Now look at me. Captain of those very men. "Well, if we had grown up in the same time, I'm sure she would have," I said grimly and then smiled, breaking the tension that suddenly built in the room. "But Maria *is* going to try to kill my mother. So, I'm going to find Peter Easton's hidden treasure and then sail to England and save her. You can come, you can stay. It's entirely up to you." My words were for all of them, but my eyes flickered to Lottie who still hung around the back, pacing behind the men. She glanced over their shoulders and met my gaze. I wished I could read her mind.

Henry stood by my side and held my hand tight. "I go where you go, remember?"

I lit up with love for the man and I squeezed his hand back. "This time, just hold on to me, okay?"

He chuckled and leaned into my face, resting his forehead against mine. "I'll never let you go again."

Everyone moaned, and Finn growled some Scottish words I couldn't understand. "Git a room, would ye?"

"Okay," I asked around, pulling away from the lure of Henry. "Are you in?"

Finn and Gus exchanged looks and both looked at

me with devilish grins. But I was surprised when Gus replied, "This is what we were made for. If you ask me, an adventure like this is exactly what we need right now," he paused and then bowed his head slightly, still holding my gaze, "Captain."

"Aye, I'm in."

Lottie stepped forward, arms crossed tightly. I wanted her approval so bad. We were on her father's ship, about to embark on her father's last journey. She opened her mouth to speak and my heart sped up.

"Of course I'm in. I missed out on this adventure ten years ago. I'm not about to let it slip through my hands again." She spoke the words, but I could still sense the hesitancy in her face.

Perhaps it was the fact I could travel through time, or maybe that I was a Cobham. Either way, I swore, then and there, that I would never betray her trust. I would spend the rest of my days proving that I was worthy of the friendship she offered so willingly.

"It's settled then," I exclaimed. "Finn set a course for Shellbed Isle. Everyone else, get some rest. We have a long journey ahead of us." *And one epic adventure*, I added to myself.

# CHAPTER FIFTEEN

I couldn't sleep that night, my mind racing with thoughts of treasure and my mother. And everything in between. I couldn't shut my eyes, it only made the images brighter, faster, more vivid. The hot morning sun crept in through the windows of my quarters and slowly warmed my back as I sat at my desk, pouring over maps and the endless pile of captain's logs.

Was I leading my friends on a suicide mission?

I'd spent the better part of the night plotting out all the different ways it could go bad. Too many to count. We all had so much to risk, and very little to gain. If we even made it to England, we could find that we were too late. That Maria had found my mom and ended her life. Or worse. What if we made it, found my mother before The Cobhams, but the woman who raised me was just as evil as my apparent sister? Did I really want to shatter the perfect image of my mother that I'd held on to all these years?

In the stark silence of the room, I heard Henry stir. "Well, now that's a glorious sight worth waiting for."

I turned in my chair to find him laying on his side, facing me, eyes open. All my worries melted away and I jumped to my feet before sliding into bed with the pirate.

"You can see," I pointed out and held his beautiful face in my hands. His wounds were healing fast and the man I remembered began to rise to the surface again.

He crushed his lips to mine with a hunger I'd never get used to. Never wanted to. When he pulled away, my body protested.

"Yes, finally," he replied and brushed the hair from my face admiringly. "And you're just as beautiful as ever." He smiled but I knew he sensed my unease as his brow furrowed. "Were you awake all night?"

I let my body fall against him, basking in the warmth and protection it offered. "Yes, I couldn't sleep. Couldn't stop worrying."

"About what?"

I shrugged. "Everything?"

Henry pulled me even closer. "You have nothing

to worry about, Dianna."

His tender kisses began at my ear and slowly trailed down my jaw, neck, and then stopped at my shoulder where the still pink wound resided. A jagged reminder of what took me away from him. He sighed.

"I'd felt it. But, God, it pains me to see it." Goosebumps scoured across my skin as his lips brushed the tiny bumps left behind by the stitches.

My body moved against his, like two waves dancing in sync. Henry's able fingers poked under the loose collar of my nightgown and tugged it down, revealing my naked breasts. His approving moan, low, raspy, and guttural shook my core as his blonde head dipped to take one in his mouth.

Finally, he shifted his body to hover over mine and peered down at me with a devilish smirk. "I've regained my strength." He spoke the words in unison with his grinding hips, rolling into me.

Delightful moans escaped my body and I wrapped my legs around his waist to pull him closer. "Good, now make me forget all my worries, Captain Barrett."

He leaned in, pressing his warm mouth to my ear, his lips moving against my skin as he whispered, "Aye, aye, my queen."

*\*\*\**

After a sleepless morning in bed with Henry, I dragged my tired and sore body down to the mess deck for some food. The crew had already eaten and were well into their day. My cheeks flushed as I passed them on the way, their playful smirks alerting me to the fact that my quarters may not be as sound proof as I'd thought.

I found Lottie in the kitchen, cleaning up and preparing for lunch. I grabbed a fresh bun and strolled over to the sink where she was bent over a heap of dirty dishes.

"Morning," I greeted.

She stopped and smiled. "Morning? More like afternoon. Are you still finding yourself tired? That baby is takin' a lot out of you."

I lobbed off a bite. "It's not the baby stealing all my strength," I joked, surprised when I actually made her laugh. "Here, let me do these."

"Are you sure?"

"Yes, I need to do something. Feel useful."

"Dianna, you're going to be leading us across the Atlantic," she reminded me. "I hardly think you're useless." But she removed her hands from the soapy water and stepped aside.

I finished my bun and then went to work on the dirty dishes. "Yes, but—" I paused and shrugged. "You know what I mean."

Lottie nodded and busied herself with peeling potatoes at my side. "Yeah, I do. Feels good to do things with your hands."

We chatted for a while, small talk about recipes and me answering Lottie's questions about where I came from as we cleaned the kitchen and prepared the food together. It did feel good to accomplish things with my hands. I missed working at the restaurant.

"Hey, do you mind if I prepare supper tonight?" I asked.

She looked slightly offended. "Are you not happy with the food I'm cooking?"

"Oh, no!" I quickly amended. "Your food is amazing. The crew loves it. I just... cooking back home, I really miss it." I smiled with an idea. A memory, really. "And I have this special recipe that the boys love. A pasta dish. I bet you'd love it, too. Actually, you can help me, if you want. Learn it."

Her shoulders relaxed. "Okay, sure."

"I mean, or you could take some time for yourself," I poked at the idea. "You know, go hang out with the boys. Maybe spend some time with Gus. I'm sure he'd love your company." She didn't answer, just flushed red and turned away from me so I changed the subject. "Just do something fun, for yourself. I haven't seen you do that since I met you."

"Fun?"

I shrugged. "Yeah, like a hobby? Don't you have something you're good at besides cooking and cleaning?"

She was lost in thought, maybe a memory, but her lips curled up at the corners as she moved the heavy pot of potatoes to the stove. "Yeah, I have a hobby," she finally replied. "I'll show it to you someday."

I laughed. "You're a woman of mystery, Charlotte Roberts."

"You're one to talk," she quipped. "A time traveller from the Cobham bloodline? I believe you're far more mysterious than I, don't you think?"

I moved closer to her. "Does that scare you?"

"What? You being related to Maria Cobham?"

"Yeah, I mean, any of it."

She stopped and stared at me, chewing the skin of her lip much like I do when deep in thought. "No," she finally replied. "I trust you. That's what friends do, isn't it? Trust one another?"

I breathed a sigh of relief. "Yeah, it is."

Just then, the kitchen dimmed with a heavy shadow and I turned to find the large porthole void of the sunlight that had shone through it just moments earlier.

"What the—" I stepped closer, peering out. My eyes bulged. "There's a ship right next to us!"

I turned to leave but a loud boom shook through the air and Lottie grabbed my arm, pulling me down behind the counter.

"That was gunfire," she whispered. "We're being boarded."

"Well, we should go up and help them!"

"Are you crazy?" she strained not to yell. "You're my captain, my *pregnant* captain. I'm not letting you go anywhere where there are guns being fired."

"Lottie!" I protested as she hauled on my arm

when I tried to stand.

"Dianna, no!" she squealed.

I grabbed the largest kitchen knife I could find, a small machete, really. I'd left my dagger upstairs in my quarters. The knife would have to do.

"I'm going up. Are you coming or not?"

She let out a moan of frustration but grabbed a knife for herself, flipping it around in her fingers like a skilled ninja. Aghast, my eyes widened, but I didn't have time to comment as she fled the kitchen and led the way upstairs.

We ducked and hid behind a couple of stacked barrels, careful not to venture too far out to the wide-open upper deck. I could hear angry voices just a few feet away and see the tops of heads through the cracks of the wooden barrels.

"We should'a killed ye when we had the chance," Finn growled at the intruders.

I shifted behind Lottie to get a better look over her shoulder and caught the face of one of the men, the one that Finn addressed. My veins immediately filled with anger, flushing out what little fear was there. I stood, clenched the kitchen knife tightly, and took a step forward. But Lottie grabbed my hand.

"What are you doing?" she whispered.

"I know these men," I told her confidently. "It's those street pirates I told you about." She released me from her grip and stood, remaining close to my side as we joined the standoff. "Good day, gentlemen. I wish I could say it was nice to see you again."

Amos let his sword fall to his side loosely at the sight of me and grinned wide, revealing his blackened teeth. "There you are," he greeted in return. "So, it's true, then. A lady captain graces the stern of The Queen. I heard it was you, I just had to see it with my own eyes."

"Dianna," Henry piped in as he took careful side-steps toward me. "You *know* these men?"

I held my chin high, not taking my eyes off Amos who was flanked by the same two men as before. "That I do," I replied. "And I was kind enough to let them live after they attacked me in the street."

I could sense the hackles standing on the back of Henry's neck and his body stiffened. "I'd advise you get back on your own ship before I turn you into chum, sir," he warned through gritted teeth.

Amos threw his head back and cackled. "We don't want any trouble," he told us. "Just give us any gold you may have, and we'll be on our way."

"You're not serious?" I retorted. "You want our money and expect no trouble?"

Amos's cheeky grin turned into a scowl as he stepped toward me. My men crossed their swords in front of me. "Oh, I expect trouble, milady," he replied sarcastically. "I just don't want it."

My eyes flickered to the ship broadside of us. Far smaller than The Queen, but still an impressive vessel for a man who had nothing just days ago. "Where did you get the ship?" I inquired, mostly stalling.

"Oh, that?" Amos quipped, looking over his shoulder. "The Franklin. I acquired it from an old sea dog, too sickly to sail it, he was. Kind enough to bestow it upon me."

I didn't believe a word he said, and Lottie's answering gasp was enough to verify my hunch. "That's Walter Franklin's merchant boat," she whispered. "I highly doubt the old man willingly gave it to a bunch of pirates. He has three sons."

My mind raced for a solution, a way out of the situation where no one got hurt. I didn't have much time, the men were growing anxious, thirsty for blood on both sides. But I wanted to be a merciful captain, respected, but also not weak. Then it dawned on me.

"I'm not going to give you anything," I told the intruders. They drew their swords, Amos a pistol, but I held my hand up and shook my head. "But I will offer you the opportunity to work with us."

His face twisted in confusion. "Work with you?"

"Dianna, what are you doing?" Henry spoke next to me.

I leaned and whispered in reply, "Just trust me." I motioned for my crew to lower their swords and I stepped forward, showing an act of trust. "We're sailing to Shellbed Isle in search of treasure. Join us, help us, and I'll give you a third of the prize."

My crew tried to stifle their moans of disapproval. The three intruders laughed, and Amos looked to me. "Is this some sort of joke? A ploy to get rid of us?"

"No, I swear on my honor as a captain," I swallowed hard, hoping that was an actual thing, "I'm leading my crew to find Peter Easton's lost treasure."

"You've just told me where it is, what's stopping me from getting it myself?"

I grinned. "Sure, you could try. If you managed to get through the Devil's Dancing Pools alive and in one piece, you could take the chance on which of the caves the treasure *might* be in." I paused, letting it register in his mind. "Or you could join me, the one person who knows exactly which cave to choose."

"Dianna," Lottie whispered next to me, knowing that wasn't true. I looked at her, my eyes begging her to trust me.

"So, what'll it be, boys?" I strained to keep a confident face, but I was a nervous wreck on the inside. My stomach toiled with anxiety and fear for my crew's lives. I had no doubt my boys could take the three stringy pirates, but they had a pistol. And we did not.

Amos mulled it over, his beady eyes distant and contemplating as he rubbed his greasy black beard.

"I'd advise ye to take the offer," Finn added. "If ye know what's good fer ye."

Amos's demeanor quickly turned to exaggerated joy and he returned the pistol to the hilt inside his jacket. I swallowed nervously as he took a step closer. "Let's go on a treasure hunt, shall we?"

"Excellent." My hand outstretched. An offer of a

truce. "We'll work together to get the treasure. No funny business. No violence," I said. "Deal?"

He slipped his greasy hand into mine and squeezed tightly. "Deal."

They returned to their ship and readied to follow us on the short journey to Shellbed Isle. I knew my crew was skeptical, unsure of my choice, but they never questioned it. I silently thanked them for their blind loyalty as I stood above the stern, the cool ocean mist blowing in my hair. Henry climbed the stairs and sidled up next to me.

"Come to tell me I'm crazy?" I asked him.

His hand shifted to cover mine on the railing, it's warmth comforting. Reassuring. "No, I'd never question your leadership. This is your vessel, after all."

I gave him a look. "Henry, just be honest with me. Is this something you would have done?"

His expression turned serious. "No, it's not. But you're not me. You're fair and show mercy. You lead with your heart and your mind. That tells me you'll make a fine captain."

"Really?" I turned and buried my face in his chest.

Henry's long arms wrapped around my body and I felt him place a kiss on my head. "Yes, in time. When you learn to trust your own judgment. But you have a loyal, loving crew on your side." His hands held my head and tipped my face up to his before pressing our lips together. "And me."

"Ahem," a voice spoke from the top of the stairs. I broke away from Henry to find Lottie standing with her hands behind her back, the faint shape of something held within them. "I'd hate to interrupt you two, but could I speak to Dianna?"

"Of course," Henry replied and kissed me once more before heading back down to the deck and joining the crew.

I looked at Lottie. "Is everything okay?"

She nodded. "I just wanted to give you something."

"What?" I shook my head. "No, Lottie, you've given me enough—"

"I insist," she said and pulled out the object from behind her back. I stared in awe. It was a hat. A gorgeous, red leather pirate's hat. "It was my grandfather's, then my father's during their time aboard The Queen. I want you to have it."

My heart squeezed in my chest. "Lottie, this belongs to you."

"No, I never wanted to captain this ship," she told me. "I'm quite happy where I am." My friend held the garment out to me.

Hesitantly, I accepted it. The worn leather felt good in my hands as I admired the gorgeous craftsmanship. Thick brown stitching laced the edges. This hat had been worn. Loved. I raised it and placed it on my head where it settled, fitting like a glove. As if it were meant for me. In that instant, as I glanced down at my adopted red jacket and brown leather boots, a trusty dagger hanging from my side, I truly felt like a captain.

A pirate queen.

"Thank you," I said and embraced my friend.

She pulled away and smiled. "It looks good on you."

Turning together to face our crew and the wide-open sea, I was content. I sucked in the heavy ocean air, let it fill my lungs and clear my head. In that very moment, I allowed myself to be blissfully happy because once we arrived at Shellbed Isle, our lives would never be the same.

# CHAPTER SIXTEEN

We sailed all night, Amos and the crew of The Franklin close behind. The mid-morning sun was high in the sky as we bustled around the upper deck of The Queen, readying the boat we'd row to Shellbed Isle. I was nervous but determined.

Suddenly, I felt a tap on my shoulder and turned to find young Charlie. My heart warmed to see him up and about. His neck still wrapped in bandages, he was still unable to speak but got along just fine with the pad of paper I gave him. I watched as he quickly scrawled down some words.

*I come.*

"Oh, no," I told him, immediately feeling sorry for the hurt look which splashed across his face. "I have a more important job for you," I continued, hoping the idea would work. I discreetly pulled out an old pistol from inside my jacket pocket, one that I'd found in my new desk. "Here, take this. Keep it hidden. If the rowboat comes back without any of us on it, I want you to shoot the men who approach."

Charlie took it with shaky hands, worry on his face. I was asking him too much, but I hoped it wouldn't come to that.

"I need you to protect yourself and the rest of the crew," I said. "If Amos and his men come back without us, I don't even want to think about what they'd do to you." My hand lovingly squeezed his shoulder and I could see him visibly brighten with purpose. Charlie sucked in a deep breath and hid the pistol in the back of his belt before heading off to help the crew.

Finn, Gus, Lottie, Henry and I lowered the rowboat and then descended the rope ladder that hung from the ship. I sat next to Henry in the middle while Lottie took the next bench. Finn and Gus were at each end, ready to row. We bobbed on the calm waves, waiting for Amos and his men to row up next to us in their vessel.

"Alright, lead the way," Amos called over. I caught the hint of something shimmer across his face. Something sly and devious. I didn't say anything but told myself to keep a close eye on the pirate.

"Are you sure about this?" Gus leaned over and

asked me.

"Not entirely," I told him honestly. "But what choice did I have?"

"We could have taken them out when we had the chance," Finn suggested.

"No, I don't want bloodshed, if I can help it."

"Well, this is going to be interestin' then," my Scottish friend muttered.

They stuck the oars in place and began rowing. Amos's boat was never more than a few feet behind as we quickly approached the mouth of a narrow inlet. I knew from the maps Lottie's grandfather had drawn, that Shellbed Isle was actually a big rock nestled in a hidden cove at the end of some rapids. If we could brave the rough waters and get to the cove in one piece, then I was pretty confident we'd find the treasure. My hope was that my experience with white water rafting would ensure our boat survived.

Not the other one.

Our boats entered the narrow opening and we rowed along quietly. Calmly. The walls of rock on either side began to rise higher and higher, telling me that we were descending in elevation and the rapids would appear any moment. I glanced over the side into the crystal-clear water where I could see every rock, crabs scuttling underneath them, mussels growing in bushels on their sides. It was beautiful. Like peering into another world. Henry held my hand and brought it up to his lips, placing a kiss across my knuckles. He said nothing, but the action was all I needed.

Suddenly, the boat began to speed up, pushing along without the aid of the oars. Finn and Gus pulled them inside, laying them on the floor. I looked back at Amos and his crew, raised a thumb up into the air, signaling them to get ready.

"We should be approaching the rapids any second," I told the people in my boat. "It's going to be rough, scary." I slipped off my seat and sat on the floor. My friends did the same. "Just hold on with everything you got. Pull on the sides to steer us away from rocks. Use the oars if you have to."

The water became turbulent within seconds and large, jagged rocks reared their ugly heads, threatening to pull us into them. Our boat tossed back and forth as the tempestuous waves played with it and we all hung on for dear life. Lottie screamed as the boat tipped and knocked her from her place on the floor, but Gus grabbed the back of her jacket and pulled the woman back in before she could spill over the side.

I dared glanced behind us just as Amos and his boat crashed into an unforgiving rock face, the sound carrying through the air like an explosion. I watched, water drenching my own face, as their boat fell to pieces and the three pirates flailed about, swimming against the waves as the rough waters carried them toward us.

"Lassie!" Finn called to me. I turned to face the front again and my eyes widened. "We've got a problem!"

We all barrelled toward the end of the rapids which poured off the edge of the Earth. My heart jumped up into my throat as I realized we were about to drop off the top of a waterfall, with no idea of how far down it went. But then I remembered; Lottie's grandfather made it over these rapids with three treasure chests. It couldn't be too far of a drop.

"Okay, get to the back!" I yelled to my crew over the crashing sounds of water against stone. We scrambled together, huddling, bracing. Our weight did as I'd hoped, and the bow of our tiny boat raised in the air as it carried us over the edge of the waterfall. We all screamed as the small craft fell through the sky and finally landed with a hard splash in the calm waters below. My knees drove into my chest, knocking the wind out of me, and one our oars were missing. But we made it. Alive.

I worried for the baby inside of me and placed a hand over my belly, telling myself it was fine. My knees had struck my chest, not lower. It should be okay. Then, I glanced back to see that the drop was only a few meters and cringed as three flailing bodies poured over the edge close behind. The trio of pirates bobbed to the surface and then swam over to where we were pulling our intact vessel onto the sand of Shellbed Isle.

"You dirty bitch!" Amos yelled at me, drawing his sword and pointing its tip to my face. "You knew!"

Before I could even blink, Henry's giant boot lifted and heaved a hefty kick to the man's gut, sending him flying back on his ass. "You dare raise a sword to her again and I'll use it to cut your God damn head off!" He backed up then, reaching out to me with his free arm. I stepped into its embrace and glared at Amos.

The pirate scrambled to his feet and lunged toward Henry, but Finn and Gus stopped him. He was smarter than most, calculated, I could see it in his face as he took in the scene before him. There was no way the three of them were a match for us. He knew it.

Soon, Amos's face softened with a smile. A fake smile, but a temporary offering of peace, nonetheless. He sheathed his weapon and held his hands up in surrender.

"My mistake," the man said. "I'll be sure not to let my anger get the best of me again."

I nodded. "You'll do well to remember that." I looked around us, observing the secret location we fell into. Shellbed Isle, the large and grassy mound no more than a hundred feet wide, sat in the center of a circular cove of calm water. Its sandy beach line was littered with broken shells and I knew then where it adopted its name from. Jagged walls of rock towered above us. And I realized, my heart jumping into overdrive as fear coursed through my veins... there were no caves in sight. Lottie seemed to make the same assessment and came over to me.

"Where are the caves?" she whispered.

"I don't know," I told her. "Maybe on the other

side of the island?"

"What's the holdup?" Amos called over to us.

Henry sensed my unease and came over, but everyone else followed. We stood around in a circle. Six pirates, a barmaid, and me. I swallowed hard at the thought that we may never get out of there.

"We're looking for some caves," I told them all. "I'm thinking they're located on the back end of the island, so let's start walking. But," I sucked in a deep breath through the nose, unsure of my next words, "this is the part that's apparently protected by sirens, so keep an eye out."

"Sirens?" Amos chortled. "What else aren't you tellin' us?"

I quirked an eyebrow at the man. "What, are you scared?"

"Of a bunch of silly fairy tales?" he guffawed. "Not likely. Lead the way."

We trekked the short distance across the small island, Henry close to my side. The simple nearness of him gave me strength and courage. Amos and his men trailed behind us, Finn close on their heels with his sword drawn, ready to catch them if they tried anything behind my back. I was so thankful for my amazing crew, my friends. Protectors. I truly felt invincible with them by my side.

We neared the water's edge on the opposite side of the island, the side you couldn't see from where we first arrived. But my stomach dropped as my eyes scanned the area and still found no caves.

"Shit..." I muttered under my breath, still not believing it. I began to suspect the stories weren't true. Or maybe Lottie's grandfather really did hide the treasure over near Corner Brook. In which case, we were doomed. Tears bubbled to the surface, and I refused to cry in front of these men. But I felt defeated. I felt like an idiot for leading them all there. I was about to turn and admit my failure when something in the water caught my eye. A strange movement, unnatural, nearly invisible to the naked eye. Or an eye that didn't know what to look for.

I took a careful step toward the water's edge, but Henry grabbed my arm. "What are you doing?" he asked in alarm.

"Shhh," I told him and gently pulled away. My eyes scanned until they found the movement once again, an invisible being made of water watching us intently from just below the surface. It was like spotting a clear jellyfish moving in the waves. You don't see it until you... *see* it.

"Hello?" I called to it and bent down to dip my fingers in the water, inviting it over. I saw the shimmer, like a heat wave, dive below the surface and swim toward me. And then, to my surprise, felt it take my hand. I remained calm and gently pulled upward, a human-like form comprised of water rose as I did so. Gasps of shock and disbelief resounded from over my shoulder, but I just stared in awe at the magical being that held my hand.

"You," it said, the sound coming from all around.

Just like it did that fateful night. "Time traveller."

My eyes widened. "Wait, how —"

Water shimmered across her form and I witnessed it fill with color. Delicate scales of peach and green, blinking eyes as blue as the deep ocean. Her hair, long and winding, made of seagrass. She finally met my gaze and grinned, showing a mouth full of pointed corals.

"The sea has and always will remain. It exists beyond the realms of time, and I exist within it. Of it."

I just stared in awe. I'd never get used to the sheer marvel that is magic. My life has been touched by it in so many ways, probably more than I even know.

"Thank you for sending me back," I told the siren. "But I'm afraid I need your help again."

She released my hand from her wet grip. "Is that so? And what do you request of me?"

"We're searching for some caves. They're supposed to be here."

"Oh," the siren replied, "Is that so? And why do you seek these caves?"

Lottie sidled up next to me, her eyes glistening with wonder. "Treasure. We seek treasure."

The creature cocked her head to the side and inhaled deeply the air around Lottie. Her eyes fluttered open and the deep pools of blueish green glimmered with recognition. "Your blood has been here before."

Lottie's cheeks flushed with crimson, her eyes

gawking. "My father!" she said in a desperate rush. "he came here ten years ago. You saw him?"

"His body poured over the falls, yes."

She couldn't keep them back any longer. her tears streamed down. "Then it's true," she spoke through blubbery lips. "He did die."

"But you knew that," I said, confused.

Lottie wiped her face with both hands and composed herself, shaking her head to clear it of emotions. "Yeah, I did. But part of me always wondered if maybe he just ran off. Or was taken." She shrugged, helpless. "You know?"

I nodded. I knew exactly what she meant. We never did find my mother's body, and I finally knew why. But all those years, logic told me she had drowned. She was dead. But a part of me always held on to the maybe, the perhaps, the... hope.

Amos pushed through the crowd of men and came to stand next to Lottie. I felt Henry tense at my side, but I held his hand firmly. "Gaw! Enough with all this glabberin' on! Where's the God damn treasure?"

The siren, perturbed by the disheveled pirate, returned to the water. I watched as her lower half resumed its translucent appearance while the rest of her remained visible. Beautiful. "The caves you seek are hidden. And the treasure is protected. Why should I lead you to them?"

"Please," I begged her. "I need it to save someone dear to me."

"So, you have noble intentions?" she asked. I

nodded. "I already granted you a wish, Time Traveller. For nothing in return. This time I require a token."

"A token? What do you mean?"

Henry leaned in and whispered. "Be careful, Dianna. The Fae are fickle and twisted. She could very well lead you to your death with a slight of words."

I cast my eyes back out to the water. "What exactly do you want from me?"

Her toothy mouth twisted into a grin, accompanied by a strange and devious look I'd yet to witness her make. It made me uneasy. "I ask nothing of you right now. But I shall call on you in the future. It could be tomorrow, it could be on your deathbed. But I will call, and you will answer. Agree, and I'll lead you to the caves."

I chewed my bottom lip in thought. I didn't like the idea of agreeing to something I had no knowledge of. She could ask me for anything in the world and I'd have to oblige.

"Dianna, don't do this. We'll find another way," Henry begged me.

But there was no other way. Maria was on a warpath to my mother, with a decent head start on us. I had Amos and his crew of pirates, thirsty for my blood if I didn't hold up my end of the bargain. I inhaled deeply. "Fine. I accept."

"Dianna!" Henry said angrily.

I shrugged and shook my head, pleading him for forgiveness. "We don't have a choice."

"There's always a choice," he replied, eyes glistening.

My heart tightened in my chest at his pain. "Not that I can see. I'm sorry." I turned to the siren. "Show us to the caves."

We all watched as the sea creature raised herself up and then dove back down into the water with a splash, creating massive ripples as she did. Just like the night I came back. Only this time, instead of creating a giant whirlpool to suck us into oblivion, the water from our feet to the rock wall which surrounded the tiny island parted. The water rose above us, suspended in time. As if invisible glass walls held it in place so we could walk through to where two cave mouths were revealed.

"Come on!" I called to everyone and we entered the chasm.

Just as we reached the entrance of both caves, the siren stepped out of the water next to us and resumed her terrifying, yet beautiful mermaid-like form. "Two choices. One will lead you to the treasure. The other will take you back out to the Earth above."

"Which one do we pick?" I asked.

The siren didn't answer, and I watched as she stepped back through the wall of suspended water, disappearing in an echo of crazed laughter.

"Great," Finn called out with a moan. "This is just lovely."

Amos stared down at me in despise. "You said you knew which cave."

"Watch it," Henry warned him and the pirate backed away.

I glanced back and forth between the two dark mouths, trying to decide which to choose. They were identical in every way, no determining difference. Both were near-perfect circles, about ten feet in diameter. Neither even had a glimmer of light from the sun on the other side, which told me the one which was an exit was probably a long way out. But I had to choose, and I had to do it fast.

"It's the one on the right," Lottie piped up.

I leaned and whispered low. "How do you know?"

"I don't," she whispered back. "But I remember my father always saying that the right one is always the right one. He used it for everything. The silliest motto, really, when you think about it. Of course, the right one is correct." She stared at the dark holes before us. "But what if the right one is truly the *right* one?"

I could have kissed her beautiful face right there in front of everyone. Pirates and their curious ways, their twisted words, and riddles. I knew then, the cave on the righthand side had to be the correct one.

"Finn, can you grab that stick right there?" I removed the white scarf I wore around my neck and wrapped it tightly around the tip of the stick and then lit a match to it. I held the homemade torch in my hand as I led the way into the cave, and hopefully to our treasure.

The cavity seemed to incline slightly the deeper

we went. We trudged along quietly, the only sounds were that of our labored breaths and slick footsteps on the wet, rocky floor. I admired the way the firelight made the damp stone glisten and the brown seaweed that hung from the tops appear alive. Like lazy tentacles. Finally, we came to the end. A solid wall of stone.

And no treasure.

"No!" I cried desperately as I felt the jagged surface in front of us.

"What kind of trickery is this?" Amos spoke angrily. "Why lead us to a dead end?"

"Mind yourself," Henry warned him and stepped close beside me. The dimming fire highlighted the worry on his face and I knew what he was thinking. What now? "Perhaps the treasure has just been claimed by someone else. There was no way of knowing that."

I felt like crying. Or screaming. Anything to relieve myself of the guilt and fear that possessed my body. I turned around in the spot I stood, anxiously searching for a secret door or a flashing light that said *enter here*! I let out a huff of frustration and threw my back against the wall in defeat, yelping as I fell through a curtain of seaweed and down a narrow hole.

"Dianna!" I heard Henry scream.

I hit the bottom of the tunnel with a hard smack, my skull bouncing off the rocky floor. My head spun as I moved to my feet. I was barely able to stand in the tiny cavity. And it was pitch dark.

"I'm okay!" I called up to everyone above. I fished another match from my jacket pocket and flicked it across a rock. The tiny flame lit the hollow which held me, and I squealed in delight at what shared the space with me. Three small chests.

And one skeleton.

The match burned out and I tossed it on the ground before lighting another. "It's here!" I yelled up to them. "The treasure is down here! Toss me a rope!"

The sounds of joyous laughter echoed through the cave a few feet above my head and my heart beat wildly with excitement as I hauled it closer to me, careful not to disturb the poor soul who'd been trapped there all those years. I tied the rope around the chest in a criss-cross fashion.

"Okay, haul it up and toss the rope back down!"

After the third one was hoisted, I bent to place my hand over the face of the skull and said a silent prayer for the fallen pirate. Hopefully, his soul could rest in peace. There wasn't much more I could do. I then wrapped the rope around my wrist and climbed the narrow tunnel back up to my awaiting friends. The rough, jagged rock surface of the narrow space tore at my hands but I didn't care. My body was flooded with adrenaline. When I reached the top, I swung a foot through the hole and pushed myself out, landing on my feet. I stood tall and flipped my straggly curls from my face as I turned to my companions, but all joy fled from my body at the sight before me.

"What the hell is going on?" I demanded to know. Amos and his two men had gaged and tied Henry and Gus. Finn had been knocked unconscious and his massive body laid on the ground while one of the men held Lottie in place, her arms tight behind her back as she struggled against his hold.

"You should have known," Amos replied. "Never trust a dirty pirate. I thought to kill you anyway, treasure or no treasure."

He bent down and smashed one of the chest's corroded locks with the hilt of his sword. The lid opened with a rusty creek to reveal more treasure than I ever thought imaginable. Coins, pearls, jewels. All sitting atop of a bed of gold coins. It was all in there and glistened like sleeping gems in the dim light of the torch fire.

"But I much prefer to walk away with the prize."

"You have no honor then?" I spat. "I was going to share the treasure with you, Amos!"

"Why would I settle for one chest when I can possess all three?" He cackled a gurgled smoker's laugh and motioned to his men. "Grab the chests. Tie these two up and let's get out of this wretched place."

I was about to protest, to fight them for the treasure we worked so hard to find. But, to my utter surprise, Lottie beat me to it. The very second Amos's henchman released her arms, I watched as she drove an elbow deep into his gut, sending him reeling over. She brought her knee up and smashed his face against it before grabbing his sword and swung it around in her hands like something straight out of a movie.

"You'll be leaving this cave a dead man if you dare move another inch," she warned Amos.

He appeared as alarmed as I was but pointed his sword right at her, ready to fight. "If you think I'm going to let a woman keep me from leaving here with these chests, then you'd be mistaken." I caught the quick flicker of his eyes at his conscious deckhand and then over to where I stood. I knew then, he was coming for me.

"Stay away from me!" I backed up as the pirate lunged toward me. Just a few feet away, his able sidekick duked it out with Lottie. But I knew then, my friend could defend herself. I, on the other hand, wasn't as lucky.

The sounds of swords clashing defended my ears in the small echo of the cave as I yanked my trusty dagger from my side with shaky hands. Behind my attacker, Henry and Gus wriggled against their ties, eyes bulging, desperate to break free and save us. I felt sorry that they had to watch the horrid scene about to unfold in front of them. My attacker took a wide swipe at me and I clumsily raised my weapon up to block it, the sharp blade just inches from my face. The sheer force that he exuded in one arm was nearly enough to bring me to my knees.

Nearly.

I held my ground and pushed my blade hard against his. "Why won't you listen to reason? We can share it, and no one has to get hurt!"

"You truly expect me to believe that?" he replied and finally retreated his sword as he stepped back, readying himself for the next blow. "After I've shown my true colors? No one is that merciful."

"I swear!"

Amos lunged one more time and I barely dodged the second swipe of his sword. His body came crashing into mine and I pushed against him with all my might. Before I could react, the man fell down the narrow hole I'd just crawled out of. In the same moment, Lottie brought her foe to his knees. A sword to his neck.

My chest heaved with quick, heavy breaths. Adrenaline burning hot through my veins. "Is *that* your secret hobby?" I asked my friend, still shocked at what I witnessed her do.

Her sword remained at the man's neck as she stole a glance over her shoulder at me and shrugged nonchalantly. "Among other things."

I shook my head, snapping back to reality as I ran over to Henry and Gus. "Yeah, you're definitely the more mysterious one." I knelt down, released them from their ties and gags. Gus immediately dove for Finn. "Are you guys alright?"

Henry grabbed my jacket and pulled me toward him, our bodies smashing together as his arms held me a little too tightly. "My God, that was pure torture." His mouth found mine and locked on. I could feel the desperation and relief seeping from his pores, in his rapid breathing, and I understood. I felt the same. "I don't know what I would have done."

My hands covered his as they held my face firmly. "It's okay," I assured him. "I'm fine." My head turned and looked down at the three chests at our feet. "Henry, we did it."

His answering smile was enough for me. "That we did."

"What do we do about these three?" Gus asked. His foot nudged the first man Lottie knocked unconscious, Jack, and looked at her with a sort of admiration.

I hopped over to the hole in the wall and peered down into the darkness.

"Amos?" I heard him moan, probably waking up from a brief blackout. I knew how far down it was. He'd be fine. I turned around to face my small crew and the one man of Amos's left conscious. "Listen carefully," I spoke to him. He was a tall, broad man. Balding at the top but sported a bushy beard that hung from his face. He glared up at me but never replied. "We're leaving here with the treasure. You could have cooperated. You could have played nice. But you ruined your chances at any of it now."

"You'd leave us here to die?" he spat.

"I should," I threatened. "It's what you guys would do, isn't it?" He didn't say otherwise. "But, no, I won't leave you here to die. I'm not heartless."

I grabbed the rope that had hauled myself and the chests out of the tiny cavity and wrapped it into as many knots as I could. "I'll leave this at the mouth of the cave. Wait until you're sure we're long gone." I narrowed my eyes at the man and then grinned. "Follow us and I'll set Lottie after you." I squat down so our faces were eye-level, for my next words I really wanted to resonate with the pirate. "And be sure to tell your friends, when you do escape this cave with the life I so graciously spared, that The Pirate Queen is a merciful captain. But I am *never* to be crossed. Do you understand?"

He refused to reply.

I glanced up at Lottie, who still held the sword to his throat, and nodded. The man winced as the sharp edge pressed tighter to his skin. "*Do* you understand?" I repeated.

"Y-yes," he finally offered.

I stood tall, hovering over him. "Good." I turned and walked back to Henry, Lottie following close behind.

"We'll find you," he dared to tell me. I spun around and stared incredulously. "We'll climb out of this cave and hunt you to the ends of the Earth. Amos won't let this go. He'll demand blood."

Before I could respond, Henry took a few steps toward the kneeling man and glared down at him with those black, soulless eyes. The ones I thought were long gone. A slight chill crept up my spine at the sight of the emptiness he so easily displayed. As if he slipped on an old mask.

"Come find us, then. I welcome it." He raised his boot and slowly pushed the man's face down to the ground, holding it there. "But the blood that's shed shall not be ours."

We all stood around in silence, shocked by Henry's sudden dark demeanor that revealed itself. I couldn't help but wonder if this was what Gus meant, about the way Henry was before my arrival. My ears began to ring as my blood heated with fear and worry that something was wrong with my beloved. What had really happened to him back there on Kelly's Island? I took a careful step forward and touched my hand to his arm.

"Henry."

He didn't respond, as if he stood in another world, unaware of the one around him.

Finally, as if a light had been turned on inside of him, he retrieved his foot and came to me. "Let's go."

Hesitantly, we gathered the chests and a barely conscious Finn before heading back the way we came. I felt a rush of power wash over me and fill my veins. Every nerve was on fire with both excitement and fear. I did it. I led my crew to an enchanted location and found Peter Easton's treasure. The people of my time would spend decades searching, but they'd never find it. A small part of me snickered at the thought.

But some other part, deep in the back of my mind, worried about the man I loved. He walked beside me, and I dared steal side glances at him, fearful. I searched for any sign of the darkness but only found that he brightened the further we walked. He caught me staring and only smiled, softening my fears until I felt silly for having them at all. Henry was just being protective back there. Angry for what Amos and his men did to us.

The siren was long gone, nowhere to be found when we emerged from the dark abyss. The water remained parted and our exit still accessible. It took a while, but we finally climbed out of the second cave as the setting sun cast a magical orange and purple glow over the cliffs of Shellbed Isle. I inhaled deeply the sweet scent of buttercups and fresh ocean mist. To me, it would always smell like victory.

We laid the heavy chests down and then collapsed on the wet grass. I knew we could only steal a moment to rest. Amos and his men would surely be close on our heels and that was a fight for another day. But I wanted to revel in the sweet high of triumph for as long as I could. My heart still racing, my veins still hot with adrenaline, I let out a fierce cry of laughter to skies above. Soon, my friends followed suit and we cackled to the heavens like a bunch of drunken jackals.

I was blissfully happy. I had everything I could ever hope for. Friends, family, a child growing inside of me and a man to share my life with. My victories. My heart. We had a long and dangerous journey ahead of us. One that would drag us across the Atlantic for months and surely test the boundaries of our close bonds with one another.

I rolled over and crushed my body to Henry's,

placing a warm kiss on his waiting mouth and then smiled. All evidence of his dark side that had reared its ugly head long melted away. A small part of me still worried about what I had seen, but I was too elated to let it bother me anymore.

"Are you okay?" I asked him.

Henry lifted his head and his mouth spread wide. "Of course," he replied. "You're safe. That's all that matters to me."

He sat up straight then and reached for the closest chest, the one Amos had busted open. I grinned as I watched him drag it over to where we sat on the dewy grass and open it up. The old lid lifted with a rusty cry and there were the sleeping jewels once again. I marveled at their beauty, their otherworldliness. Blue sapphires too large to hold in one hand, emeralds and rubies so saturated in color they looked like expensive Christmas ornaments. Henry stuck a hand in the treasure and scooped out a fistful of gold coins.

"This is ours, Dianna," he told me with delight. "We have the world in our hands and nothing to stop us."

"Stop us from what?" I asked, still dancing around the thought of the darkness I worried still resided within him. I'd been so elated to finally have him back that I never stopped to really see. To truly look at the man I'd pulled out of that room on Kelly's Island.

His eyes flickered with... something. I wasn't sure. A shadow. An emotion, or lack thereof. But it melted away within seconds and my Henry resurfaced once again. He tossed the coins back in the chest and scooted closer, taking me in his arms. My head tipped back as I looked up at his beautiful face, tracing the lines of his sharp jaw and flushing the worries from my mind once again. No, this man was a pirate who'd been through a great ordeal. He would always be my Henry.

I reached up and brought his face down to mine, placing a kiss on the side of his mouth. "I love you."

I felt his face move with a grin. "And I you, Time Traveller." He pulled away to gaze into my eyes and I found myself lost in his deep, dark pools. They glistened with love for me and I returned to my blissful joy over our victory. His eyebrows raised. "Now, shall we go to England?"

I laughed. "Yes," then craned my head to our friends who were adoring the contents of the other two chests. "To England!"

"Aye, aye, captain!" they called back in unison and laughter.

It didn't matter how impossible the journey ahead would be. I wasn't scared of facing Maria or of what I'd discover if we did find my mother. I didn't fear what the sea had in store for us or the fact that I would be giving birth in a few months. I could face it all.

As long as I had Henry by my side.

# THE END

Continue the epic tale of Henry and Dianna's adventure with book three in The Dark Tides series, **The Blackened Soul**, available wherever books are sold and read on for a look at chapter one!

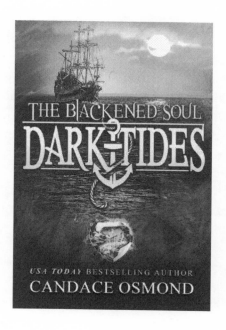

Nearly three months at sea with your best friend and a crew of burly pirates sounds like an adventure until you're secretly fearing for your life in the dead of night. I wrapped my red coat tightly around my shift, blocking out the chilly night air as I stood on the deck above the stern.

I leaned against the thick wooden railing as I peered down at the mesmerizing midnight sea below and watched the dark tones of jade crash together while my ship trailed along on our never-ending journey to England. I found myself in that same spot, night after night, worried for... everything. My crew, my mother, the child growing inside of me.

And Henry's sanity.

I led us on this potentially doomed mission and my friends followed blindly. Now I laid awake every night, obsessing over everything that could go wrong. Who was I to lead a crew of pirates? Who was I to think she could sail across the ocean and take down the most ruthless woman to ever exist? I knew very little of this era aside from what I'd been exposed to and I often found myself making decisions on the fly. Like saving Henry from Kelly's Island. I'd replayed the whole thing in my mind a million times and entertained all the many ways it could have gone so horribly wrong.

I was lucky, at best, and I worried when that luck would begin to run out.

"I thought I'd find you up here," spoke a voice from over my shoulder.

I turned to find Lottie and smiled. Our three months at sea brought us closer together and our friendship had grown into something I took comfort in. "Yeah, couldn't sleep."

"Again?" She sidled up next to me and rested her forearms on the railing. "You may be able to evade sleep," she reached over and placed her palm against my slightly curved belly, "but that baby cannot. Go to bed, Dianna."

"Why are you up?" I asked, dodging her demand.

She shrugged. "I worry about you. Ever since—"

"Don't," I told her and mindlessly reached up to touch my fingers to my throat, the skin still tender from the remnants of bruising I hid with a scarf. "Forget I told you about that."

She opened her mouth to protest but I shot my friend a look that said it was over. Lottie then sighed and looked up at the twinkling stars above us. "Augustus is worried about Henry."

"Why? What did you tell him?"

I caught a slight roll of her eyes. "Nothing. You know I'd never speak a word of sworn secrecy, Dianna."

"Yeah, I'm sorry," I replied, immediately regretting my words. "You're right. I shouldn't have said that." I inhaled deeply. "I'm just becoming stir crazy."

"Finn says we should be there soon."

"God, I hope so." I folded my arms tightly across my torso and gazed up with her. "I love the sea.

But I'm ready to step foot on some land for a while."

"I would sell my soul for a warm bath," she spoke dreamily.

I found myself laughing, something I hadn't done in a while. Not sincerely, anyway. "And a fresh pot roast."

We sat on a wooden crate and listed the many things we'd delight in once we made landfall. Clean clothes, a long bath, a comfy bed, favorite foods. The list went on until the faint orange-red glow of the rising sun began to seep through the low clouds on the horizon. My signal to head back to my quarters. Where Henry slept, unaware of where I spent most of my nights. Lottie and I parted ways and I turned the old brass knob to my room, careful to be as quiet as possible.

But it didn't matter.

"Up early again, I see," he spoke solemnly. I turned to find him standing at the window, gazing out at the same ocean I'd been staring at earlier. He spun slowly and met my eyes, his full of regret and pain. I looked away, as I often did. Ignoring it.

"Lottie couldn't sleep," I lied and went straight to my bed.

"Oh?" Henry mused and walked toward where I sprawled out across the blankets.

His large frame cast a shadow over my body and a chill crept up my spine. He then kneeled next to the bed, allowing the morning sun to shine over his shoulders and warm my face as he placed a careful hand on my growing belly.

"Is she alright?"

"Yes," I continued to fib. My white lies were beginning to pile up, and I feared when they'd turn black. "Just restless. Eager to get off the ship."

He nodded mindlessly. "Yes, as we all are." His wide hand fanned over the slightly curved shape of my stomach and the hint of a smile found its way to his lips. "How is baby today?"

The life growing inside of me had become the only topic we could comfortably talk about. Something we both shared and loved fiercely.

"Quiet," I told him and mirrored the tiny smile. "We should probably think of a name, something besides *baby*."

His brow furrowed. "But we don't know whether it's a boy or a girl."

"We could pick a gender-neutral name," I suggested.

Henry's face warped in confusion. "Gender-neutral?"

"Uh, yeah, sorry." I laughed. "That's a term from my time. It means something that works for all genders. Male, female, or any other."

His face remained twisted in thought as he processed my words. "Any *other*?"

I laughed again and leaned over to smooth the surface of his scruffy cheek with my hand.

"Yes, but that's a conversation for another time. I don't want to overload your old-world brain."

The moment was light, but I immediately took note of how his body relaxed into my touch as if he'd been too scared to touch me first. The thought struck a chord in my heart. I pulled at the collar of his white shirt and brought his face to mine.

"Kiss me, Henry."

His body was tense, unsure, but did as I asked. The warmth of his soft lips melted mine and I breathed in the scent of him. Sweat and sleep mixed with something else. Something that always lured me in and clouded my judgment. Like a siren's song, Henry's very existence called to me. Over threads of space and time. He was my soulmate... no matter how dark his soul may be.

His chest vibrated with a deep moan as he shifted to hover above me on the bed. His long legs spread mine open and I grabbed his thick leather belt, driving his hips into me. A warm shiver coursed through my body as his mouth found my ear and he whispered deeply.

"God, how I've missed you."

I tilted my head back in ecstasy, body writhing against his. "I'm right here. I've always been right here."

Henry paused and pulled away, looking into my eyes, his glistening with threats of tears. In them, I could see so much pain, so much regret, and I felt his torment. Gently, I grabbed his face and touched my forehead to his.

"Dianna—"

"Shh, don't," I whispered. "You don't have to. It's okay."

"No, it's not," he argued and removed himself from atop my body to stand next to the bed, his back facing me.

"Henry, please," I begged. "Don't retreat again. Stay with me."

"How can you say that? How can you still want me?"

"What do you mean? That's all I want. For things to go back to the way they were before—" I had to stop myself. I refused to speak the words. To give them life.

But Henry spun back around and faced me with a fiery intensity blazing in his eyes. His fists tight balls at his sides. In that moment, I knew he was gone again and there was nothing I could do to reel him back. "What? Before I nearly killed you?"

"Henry," I replied and stood. "You didn't."

"The marks you hide say otherwise."

My throat tightened at the memory that forced its way through. But I shook my head. "You didn't know what you were doing. You were sleeping."

"Was I?" he replied, eyes gone dark. Empty. "Then how come I remember it all? My hands around your..." He brought his palms up and stared at them in disgust. "I shouldn't be anywhere near you."

I took a step toward him, but he retreated. "Just let me help you. You can't live like this. *We* can't live like this."

"How can you possibly help me?" he asked as he hastily grabbed his belongings and shoved on his black leather jacket.

"By talking about what happened to you on that damn island!"

His head shot up and his dark, soulless eyes bore into mine. "No."

"Henry—"

"No!" he bellowed. The man stood there for a moment, chest heaving in anger before he stormed out of our quarters and slammed the door behind him. He left me there in the stone-cold silence that had quickly become my life. The sound of my heartbeat, hot and rapid in my ears, the only noise to be found. I allowed a moment to fall apart before I forced myself to gather up the pieces and step into my daily role as captain. My crew needed me.

I just wished Henry needed me, too.

***

The vibration of our swords colliding pulsed down my arm and radiated deep in my bones. But it was a sensation I'd grown to like. Love, even. Finn had been seriously teaching me to use a sword for weeks now, and I looked forward to our daily lessons. They were one of the few things that removed me from the despair I felt with Henry's PTSD.

Finn lunged at me, sword swinging hard from side to side. I dodged the blade with ease and brought my own up to block it. His face grinned madly. "Aye, yer catchin' on fast, Lassie."

"I would hope so, we've been at this for weeks," I replied breathily and pushed against him.

"Some take years to master their blade," he told me as we danced around one another in our practiced positions. "Some never truly grasp it at all."

"Well, I need to know how to defend myself."

"Aye, I won't argue against ye there." He spun around and flung his blade down low. But I caught it, hooking mine around it in a twirling fashion and forced it up and away from me. "But it would have been easier to teach ye to use a pistol, I reckon."

The thought of using a pistol on anyone didn't sit well in my stomach and the image of the barrel pointing at Henry flashed through my mind so fast I barely caught it. I shook my head, but the ashes of anger coursed through my veins and I used that to fuel my swinging arm. My fingers gripped the hilt tightly and I pushed against the space that Finn occupied, forcing him into a corner and held the edge of my blade to his neck. His eyes bulged at the sudden defeat.

"I'll do just fine with a sword," I told him and let it drop to my side as I backed away.

"Clearly," he replied and coughed. An awkward silence hung in the air between us. "Uh, did ye want to get some breakfast? I think we can still catch it before Lottie cleans up."

I forced a smile for my friend. "Sure."

We descended the ladder to the mess deck and found a couple of the deckhands still hanging around, their plates empty but the conversation full as they enjoyed a cup of tea. But they both came to a respective halt at the sight of me. I rarely made an appearance in the morning because I often used those hours to catch up on sleep while Henry stepped in as captain for me.

"Please," I said to them, "Don't stop because I'm here. Enjoy your tea."

They tipped their hats and smiled at me as I took a seat at an empty table. Finn ducked into the kitchen area where Lottie no doubt would be found. I rubbed my tired eyes and raked my fingers through the tangled mess of hair that sat on my shoulders. My mind raced with concern for the man I loved. He had to get a handle on his PTSD.

I just wished he'd let me help him. After my mom's apparent death, Aunt Mary encouraged me to see a psychiatrist. I refused at first, determined to deal with my emotions in sullen silence. But, once I did, when I finally opened up and began to purge my feelings, I started to heal. It was a slow process, but it worked.

I knew that losing my mother at a young age couldn't even be compared to what Henry went through in his lifetime. The savagery, the loss, the torture. Maria Cobham twisted his mind and soul until he could barely recognize himself in the mirror. He even became a whole other person in the process; Devil Eyed Barrett. But I had to hold on to the hope that if he just opened up to me, talked about what happened, then perhaps he could find his own way to heal.

Finn emerged from the kitchen with a tray full of food for us. "There's not much left, but I scrounged up some grub." He sat down on the bench seat across from me and shoved the tray in my direction. "Eat, ye look like ye needs it."

"Thanks," I replied with a smile. I grabbed a mug of tea and lifted it to my mouth, letting the warmth seep into my mouth and nose. After a few sips, I moved onto the bowl of porridge my friend offered and tossed a couple of spoonfuls into my mouth.

"I still prefer yer cookin'," he admitted as he gobbled up the pale slop.

"Yeah, I know," I replied. "But Lottie does a great job. Being the ship's cook gives her a purpose she loves."

"Oh, I don't mind the lassie's food," he quickly amended. "It's edible." A grin splashed across his face. "But I'd give me right arm for one of them buns of yers."

I tried to stifle the laugh that erupted from my gut, but such a thing was impossible around Finn. I'd hate to see the state I'd be in if I never had friends like him and Lottie to take comfort in. "I can make some later today if you really want them that bad." I threw him a wink. "You can keep your arm."

Finn waggled his bushy red eyebrows as he held the bowl up to his mouth to slurp the rest of his porridge. He then downed an entire cup of tea in one gulp and rubbed the remnants of food and beverage from his long beard with the palm of his hand.

"You know, I could give you a shave, if you want," I offered.

He feigned offense. "What? Cut me beard off?"

"Yeah, it must get annoying. No?"

"The day I let someone remove a hair from me face is the day I lay down and die," he half kidded.

I chuckled and ate a few more bites of the lukewarm porridge before setting it aside. "How much longer do you think we have?"

"Until we get there?" he asked. I nodded in response. "I reckon another two weeks. Maybe less. Maybe more. The sky is grey today and a chill in the air. Could be a storm comin'."

"Oh? Should I be worried?"

He shook his head. "Nah, I doubt it'd be anythin' more than some rain and gusts. Nothin' The Queen cannae handle."

I breathed a sigh of relief. "Good. But ready the rowboats and secure the deck just in case. We don't want to lose anything."

"Aye, Captain," he replied and tipped his head in a mock fashion.

I'd been captain of our ship for months now, but Finn still found amusement in my role. I let it slide because, to be honest, I felt it was a laughable thought most of the time. Me, Dianna Cobham. A wayward chef from Newfoundland captaining a full-rigged pirate ship? Yeah, I'd laugh, too.

"So, what's the plan for when we hit the shores of England?" he asked.

I sucked in a deep breath through my nose and shrugged. "I'm not sure."

"Yer not *sure*?"

"Well, I thought we'd set up somewhere," I quickly recovered. "Henry said he has a friend in Birmingham we can stay with if need be. I don't expect to find Maria immediately. I know it'll take some time, some scouting and asking around."

"Aye," he nodded thoughtfully, scratching at his beard, "and then?"

"What do you mean?"

"What do ye have in mind when we get our hands on the wench?"

I struggled to think of a response. Not because I hadn't thought of what I'd do, but because I thought of it too often. And I still didn't have an answer. Killing her felt wrong, it went against the grain of my very moral fibers. But letting her go would be an injustice to the world.

I hung my head and closed my eyes. "I don't know yet."

Finn leaned across the table and grabbed my hand gently, his voice low. "Then I suggest ye figure it out 'cause I reckon Henry has his own plans for Maria and ye may not like it."

Our eyes locked in a shared understanding, but I knew mine projected the fear that suddenly ran through my body. Henry didn't want to open up to me, didn't want to burden me with his demons... because he planned to slay them all on his own once we reached our destination. He was going to kill Maria.

The man I loved was going to murder my sister.

# ABOUT THE AUTHOR

#1 International and *USA TODAY* Bestselling Author
Candace Osmond was born in North York, ON.
She published her first book by the age of 25, the first
installment in a Paranormal Romance Trilogy to which two
others were published with it. The Iron World Series.
Candace is also one of the creative writers for sssh.com, an
acclaimed Erotic Romance website for women which has
been featured on NBC Nightline and a number of other
large platforms like Cosmo. Her most recent project is a
screen play that received a nomination for an AVN Award.
Now residing in a small town in Newfoundland with her
husband and two kids, Candace writes full time developing
articles for just about every niche, more novels, and a
hoard of short stories.

**Connect with Candace online! She LOVES to hear
from readers! *www.AuthorCandaceOsmond.com***

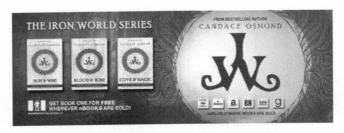

Made in the USA
Middletown, DE
20 August 2021

46484212R00144